THE SCOT'S QUEST
HIGHLAND SWORDS BOOK 4
Published by Keira Montclair
Copyright © 2020 by Keira Montclair

This is a work of fiction. Names, characters, places and inci-
dents are either the product of the author's imagination or
are used fictitiously, and any resemblance to actual persons,
living or dead, business establishments, events or locales is
entirely coincidental.

Printed in the USA.

Cover Design and Interior Format by
The Killion Group, Inc

HIGHLAND SWORDS 4

THE SCOT'S QUEST

KEIRA MONTCLAIR

PROLOGUE

Highlands, not far from Grant land

H E'D LOVED HER MORE THAN any other woman in his life and she was gone.

Madeline Grant had been the perfect woman—beautiful, sweet, loving, loyal, everything a man could want in a wife. But she'd met Alexander Grant first, and they'd married and made a life together, raising five bairns of their own and one adopted child.

But it could have ended so differently. She could have left to be with him.

He would never forget the first time they met.

Racing across the cobblestones for one of the festivals, he'd fallen down and skinned his knees. His mother and father had been far behind him, but that had proven his salvation. A yellow-haired angel had picked him up, brushed the dirt away, and said, "Dry your eyes, laddie. I'll fix you up so it will pain you no more."

Maddie had taken him inside, dressed his wounds,

and planted a soft kiss on each of his knees before she handed him back over to his mother. Ever since then, his eyes had followed her wherever she went. The mistress had stolen his heart.

As he grew from a laddie into a man, his interest in her changed. It became a kind of obsession. But the taller he grew, the less Maddie spoke to him. Still, he found every excuse he could to see her, to talk to her. Why, he'd even brushed down Alex Grant's horse whenever the chief returned from battle. Why? Because Madeline always came to offer the beast an apple.

She'd cooed and stroked that horse so much he'd needed to turn away to hide his arousal, but it had always been worth the risk.

Until that fateful day.

The darkest day of his life.

He was a man by then, with a broad, muscular body. And although she no longer sought him out or smiled at him, he had told himself it was because she was trying to avoid her own changing feelings. If he approached her now, she was sure to accept him, if only as a lover. The difference in their ages wouldn't matter.

So he'd approached her in the stables.

She had politely rejected him and suggested he leave Grant land.

The prospect of being away from her had nearly killed him, but he'd feared retaliation from the powerful laird. So he'd packed his things and left.

In the long, lonely years that had followed, he'd only had the chance to set his gaze upon the love of his life but once a year, for the chief had allowed him to visit his parents every Christmas. But they'd died years ago, taking his excuse with them, and now she was gone, too.

The ache in his heart was too large—it had only grown bigger for every year she was gone—and he'd finally made a decision.

After all these years.

After all these decades.

He was going to make Alexander Grant pay for cheating him out of the woman who should have belonged to him. He wasn't quite sure how he'd accomplish it, but he'd do it through the man's bairns and his grandbairns.

And if he lost his life over it, so be it.

CHAPTER ONE

Autumn, 1307, MacLintock Castle

DYNA GRANT STOPPED HER HORSE, handing off her game to the guards who'd ridden with her and waving them ahead. Meanwhile, she reached for her bow, ready to shoot one or both men before they caught sight of her. Two sheriffs stood arguing with her grandsire, Alexander Grant, the mighty swordsman who had now lived beyond seven decades. True, her grandfather wasn't alone—her cousins Alasdair and Els stood with him—but she was in a better position to put arrows in the sheriffs' arses if they dared to touch Grandsire.

She approached slowly, ignoring the slight breeze, the rustle of the leaves falling from the trees, the sweet smell of the recent rainfall. Normally, she would bask in the small pleasures of her ride, but not this morn.

The sheriffs might not be threatening her grandfather, yet, but the fine tic in his jaw, something she saw even from ten horse lengths away, told her their reason for traveling to MacLintock Castle would upset everything and everyone. As she got closer, she realized she knew one of the men. He'd helped Dyna and her cousins in the past, proving himself to be true to the Scots and Robert the Bruce. The other? She'd astutely doubt every word he said until he proved his value.

"Grandsire, has something happened?" she shouted, her nearly white plait bouncing across her shoulders as she approached the group.

Her grandfather waved for her to dismount.

When the two sheriffs turned their attention to her, she said, "What ill news do you bring this time? Another death that's a lie, a promise from King Edward, a garrison on its way to attack us?"

The one she trusted was Sheriff De Fry, but of course it was the other man who answered her. She'd seen him before but couldn't recall his name. She only knew she didn't like the smug look on his face. "Is this how you thank someone who's turned a favor for your clan?" he asked.

"What favor?"

De Fry said, "Sheriff Busby heard that King Edward has sent a large garrison of men out with orders to capture Alexander Grant. He is to be brought to the royal castle at Berwick. We came to advise him to go into hiding."

Her heartbeat sped up so much she feared it would explode out of her chest. Grandsire looked completely calm. Even that tic in his jaw had stopped.

Grandsire said, "My thanks to both of you for the information. We'll make our plans with that in mind."

"Where will you go?" Busby asked.

"Nowhere that I will tell you. But I intend to leave in a few days."

De Fry snorted, a smirk covering his face as he turned around and headed to his horse, ending the visit.

"I'm a Scot," Busby objected, his face red. "You can trust me."

"We'll see. I wouldn't entrust that information to many."

Busby gave the old man a final glare before he, too, climbed onto his horse and flicked the reins without another word.

Alex watched him go, his stare telling Dyna that something about the man niggled at him. Busby felt wrong to her too. Her grandsire's sense of discernment had come from a lifetime of fighting and leading, of experience, but Dyna's skills were different. She'd been born with them. Sometimes they warned her away from people who intended harm, sometimes they even gave her knowledge of the future. It had always been that way, so it was impossible to explain *how* she knew the things she knew. She only understood that she did. With some people, her intuition was so undeniable they may as well be dressed like the devil himself.

This man wasn't so clearly labeled, but she felt the warning nonetheless.

As soon as the sheriffs were out of hearing distance, Alasdair asked, "Do you believe them?" According to their elders, Alasdair was the image of Alex Grant in his younger days. He was especially close to Grandsire since his father, Jake, had passed on at a young age.

"I do," Grandsire said. "The English tried to capture me through John, then through Kyla. Both attempts failed. The new English king, Edward's son, doesn't know much about fighting, but he knows how to give orders. I'm not concerned by a few groups of Englishmen. They don't know the Highlands the way I do." He tossed the end of his red, green, and black plaid over his shoulder as if to flaunt it. Grandsire wore his Scottish pride well, and it was little wonder—he was the man who'd made Clan Grant what it was in the Highlands.

One of the most powerful clans in all the land.

"True, they'll probably never find you," Els said, his light-colored locks blowing in the breeze. "I wonder if they still think they can force our warriors to fight for England."

Grandsire nodded, then said, "We'll only discuss this again in the solar. This is not information to be disseminated to the clan. Give me time to consider all I've heard. First we eat."

He walked through the gates with his head held high, but Dyna could see his hip still pained him, as it had for the past few years. Aunt Jennie had given him salve to ease the joint pain, but it seemed to have worsened. She jumped down from her horse, pushed the animal toward a stable lad, and hurried after him.

"Grandsire," she said, catching up to him and clutching his elbow. "You know we will protect you. You decide on a strategy and we will deliver. We'll not allow the English bastards to get you. Ever." She loved to walk beside her grandsire. When she was with him, it felt like his ferocity was bolstering her own strength and will.

Once they entered the bustling courtyard, her grandfather patted her arm and gave her a look that told her to hold her tongue for now. The man was capable of commanding the largest army in the Highlands with the movement of his eyes or his head. Rarely did anyone question him—even now, many years after his sons had officially taken over the leadership of the clan.

The laughter of two bairns carried to them, putting a wide smile on the old man's face. A wee lassie and a wee laddie came racing across the courtyard.

"*Seanair*, watch this. We racing!" John, Alasdair's son, pointed to a tree a short distance away and nodded to the wee lassie next to him.

"Go!" she said.

The two ran to the tree, laughing and giggling all along the way. John touched the tree a few seconds ahead of the lass. "Coira, I won. Do again. Then you win."

Grandfather nodded, apparently satisfied with the lad's approach to his play, then kept moving. "You're a fine runner, John. Continue your practice."

Watching the bairns reminded her of her own childhood. Of the way she, Alasdair, Els, and Alick used to carry on together. Although the lads had all been born on the same night, something that had bonded them together, Dyna, born a year and a half later, had always been a part of their group. At three summers, she used to guide their games. She had always been the one to help put a stop to their bickering and battles and propel them to more *interesting* activities.

When she was about ten summers, her grandsire had told her that the lads had no idea she controlled them. From then on, she had paid attention to the way the lads played with her, and it soon became clear that he was right. They did whatever she did. One time, they had even followed her straight through a deep puddle of mud that she'd managed to side-step at the last possible moment.

Els had entered first, Alick following him in blindly. Alasdair, usually a bit more alert than the others, had caught himself just in time, saving himself from a drenching.

Alick's mother had bellowed from across the courtyard. "Alick, those were new boots you just muddied up." Alick had stopped in the middle of the muck, slightly in shock, while Els climbed out of the other side.

Grandsire's laughter had carried to her from the parapets. She had many fond memories of playing with her cousins, one of the many reasons she enjoyed watching John and Coira.

As the wee ones took off for another race, Dyna and her grandsire continued on to the MacLintock keep. Just before Grandsire opened the door, he whispered something in her ear.

"And so it begins again."

She'd been thinking the same.

Derric Corbett ended his sparring with another of Bruce's warriors, wiping the sweat from his brow. He'd removed his tunic because it was a warm day in early autumn, and he didn't wish to dirty one of the few tops he had.

"You've built up, Corbett," his sparring partner said. "Just from your swordplay?"

"Aye."

"Apurpose?"

"Aye. Have you not seen the Grant warriors? Especially the cousins? They're all bigger than any other warriors. They claim 'tis from swordplay." He grabbed a skin of ale and downed two swigs. There was a breeze at the moment, something he loved to feel across his body.

The only thing that would feel better was Dyna Grant—her hands, her breasts, her lips... Would she notice his new bulk?

That thought got a reaction from his traitorous groin, just like it always did, so he spun around and headed to the nearby burn to throw cold water on his face.

It was there Robert the Bruce caught up with him. Dark-haired and clean shaven, King Robert had a dignified look one didn't often see in a man who spent much of his time living in the forests. He looked more tired than usual, battle weary, but he was relentless in his pursuit of the claim to his title as King of Scotland. The capture of his wife and other family members showed in the lines in his face, but his eyes still demonstrated a keen mind. Their king believed in stealth and cunning over brute battle strength.

"King Robert," Derric said, nodding to him as he dipped his cupped hands into the water and threw the cool refreshment across his face and neck.

"Corbett. I was searching for you. I forgot to tell you something. A lass named Senga came looking for you when I sent you on patrol two moons ago, said she'd known you last year. She was a drifter, following my camp, but she asked specifically after you. Do you recall her?"

He stopped, remembering the lass with golden hair, bewitching green eyes, and those big…

"You know of whom I speak?" Robert asked.

"Aye. Senga. She was a sweet lass, but she had ambitions. 'Twas just a fling."

Robert shrugged. "She didn't say why she wished to see you, but after her departure, someone told me she'd spoken of her new bairn. Might it be yours?"

Derric froze. He'd tried to make sure he didn't leave a bunch of children behind, but he supposed it was possible.

What was he to do? He'd hoped to go to MacLintock Castle to see his sister and a certain tall, willowy blonde with fire in her eyes. Ever since he'd had a taste of Dyna Grant, he hadn't been able to get her out of his mind. More than once, he'd woken up in the middle of the night with a hard cock, memories of her sweet lips and fine arse drifting through his mind.

Robert the Bruce clasped his shoulder. "Senga has a wee lassie with bright-colored hair is what I was told. She was headed north into the Highlands. After she left, someone told me she was searching for the father of the bairn, though she never named you. I just wished to mention it because she asked after you. Do as you wish with the information."

The babe couldn't be his, or could it? Derric pressed his memory, trying to recall how often he'd been with the lass. They hadn't been involved for long, and he'd always been careful. Still, the babe could be his. He knew a few times was all it took.

Did he have a daughter?

Perhaps he should take the time to look Senga up. Ask her the question himself. In the meantime…

"King Robert?" he said, turning back toward the burn. The king was dipping his head under a falling stream of water cascading between a few stones. "Would it be a bother if I take a sennight or two to visit my sister? We're not far from where she's living."

"Nay, after Loudon Hill and Lorn, I don't think we'll have much to do until we get farther north. Come back though, aye? And give my best to dear Joya."

He hoped his gaze didn't give him away. True, he'd love to visit Joya, but he *needed* to see Dyna, and that need was becoming stronger every day.

Ever since his parents were slain by English soldiers eight years ago, Derric had devoted his life to making the English bastards pay for their crimes against Scotland. In many ways, it was a gratifying quest. And yet, seeing how happy Joya was with Dyna's cousin, Els, he couldn't help but wonder if a life with Dyna might be more satisfying than this endless fight for Scotland.

Or perhaps Dyna would wish to fight beside him? He thought back to the battle outside of Thane Castle when Dyna had climbed onto his shoulders and thrust her sword into the air, the crackle of thunder shaking the ground around them. The lass had uncanny talents for sure.

King Robert asked, "Is that smile for Senga?"

Embarrassed to have been caught thinking on a lass, he whipped off a lie easily. "Nay, I was thinking of Joya. I'd like to see that she's doing well with her husband."

"I'm sure she's quite happily married. Mayhap she'll give you a niece or nephew. Send her my best."

"I will." It was an easy promise to make, and Derric nodded without hesitation.

He wished Robert hadn't brought up Senga, but he doubted the bairn was his daughter. And while he intended to seek her out to ease his mind—he felt the powerful pull of a pair of ice blue eyes. A smirk of pouty lips. Dyna would shoot a challenge at him, the way she always did, and he'd be powerless to ignore it. He'd be grateful for it.

CHAPTER TWO

TWO DAYS LATER, DYNA WAS in the meadow, practicing her archery skills, when she heard the hoofbeats of a lone horseman. It was nearly dusk so it would be hard for her to identify the visitor, but she wasn't worried—instead she turned until her bow was perfectly aimed at the horseman.

He looked to be heading toward the gates, but as soon as his gaze settled on her, he turned his horse. She didn't lower the bow at first, confused because he looked so different than he had several moons ago, when he'd left MacLintock Castle, promising to return for her.

Derric Corbett.

Small butterflies fluttered in her belly at the sight of him, at the realization he'd built up his tall, lanky body during their time apart. When her gaze met his, the many moons of separation dissolved into a heat of need she didn't completely comprehend except that she liked it.

She'd always felt immune to men, until she'd met Derric Corbett. Her attraction to him was raw and wild, and it opened her up in a way she'd never experienced.

This spring, she'd coerced him into going off with her on a journey to find Coira. Her older sister Lora had run away and joined Clan MacLintock, and Lora had been desperate to be reunited with her. Their mother had passed on, and their father didn't have the time or inclination to take care of such a young child. Lora had been raising her, or near enough. So Dyna had promised to bring the wee lassie to MacLintock land.

The lassie's father had happily agreed, the old bastard.

Derric had gone with her, along with a few guards. Their trip had been uneventful, but something had seethed between them the entire time. She'd wanted to touch him, to kiss him, but they hadn't had much time alone. Until they brought Coira home. Derric had led Dyna outside to say goodbye, and he'd said it better than any other goodbye had ever been said.

With his lips.

He'd left her with a kiss—a searing, passionate kiss that had made her feel an indescribable need, something that had overpowered her senses and her reasoning. A need to taste him, to feel his hardness against her. That need had insisted on being released in some way.

But then he'd left.

He'd only been back for a few moments, and he was already affecting her the same way.

Damn it all. She would never allow herself to be

controlled by a man, even if he wasn't trying to control her.

And yet, at the same time, she had the odd urge to allow Derric to control her completely, without a speck of clothing on.

She lowered her bow as Derric dismounted in front of her, tying the reins of his horse on a nearby bush, his long blond locks swaying in the wind. The man even had an interesting hair color. Most of the time it appeared blond, but it bore hints of red on sunny days. Not nearly as red as Joya's, but still red. He strode toward her, his wide grin telling her that he recalled the way they'd parted as clearly as she did. Did he feel the same strange rush of heat?

Then she couldn't help it. Her gaze raked over his body from his handsome head to his toes. Hell-fire, the quirk of his brow said he'd caught her. Had she no shame?

"I see you're as pleased to see me as I am to see you." He stopped in front of her, his green eyes searching every part of her, then he set his hands on her shoulders. Leaning forward, he lowered his lips to her ear and whispered, "Just say aye, lass."

She wanted to deny him, if only because he was so infuriating, but instead she found herself leaning toward him. Reaching for him.

His response was a growl as his arms wrapped around her, tugging her so close that their bodies melded together. She yanked him closer, whimpering with delight when his mouth finally met hers, his tongue stroking hers.

She gave him better than she got. His response was to lift her off the ground and hold her against his body, so close that she could feel his hardness through the rough fabric of his trews. Her nipples peaked, begging to be set free of their constraints.

He ended the kiss, and as a last attempt to save face, she pushed against him and said, "Enough."

He winked. "I don't for one moment think 'twas enough for you. I see you haven't forgotten our last meeting either."

Her gaze narrowed, and he took the warning for what it was, stepping out of her reach. "Now be nice, Diamond. I know you're happy to see me. I assume you don't greet everyone like that."

"Nay, I don't. And why do you still insist on calling me that?" She wasn't sure whether to be offended by his pet name for her.

She crossed her arms to keep from reaching for him.

"Diamonds are the most beautiful jewel of all, are they not? The clearest and the hardest."

"And I'm clear and hard?"

"Clear? Nay, that word is all wrong for you. Mysterious and beautiful fit you better, so mayhap I should call you sparkly. Hard? Well, let's just say you're tough to take down. I've yet to see any tears, and most women I know cry when a drop of rain hits them. Tough would be a more accurate description. Does that offend you?"

She pursed her lips, chewing over his answer. To be called tough was, to her mind, a better compliment than beautiful. "Nay, you have not offended me, but 'sparkly' is not a word I'd use to describe myself."

"Well, I'm rather fond of my name for you."

She gave him a light tap on his shoulder with one of her arrows, something he probably didn't even feel through the thick fabric of his tunic. Then she glanced up and down his body, pleased to see her first assessment had been correct. Derric had been working hard to build his upper body size and strength.

"Enough jesting," she said, tearing her gaze away from his body. "Why are you here?"

"I came to visit my sister…and you. Is that not allowed?" he asked, setting his stance wide and crossing his arms. "She is here, is she not?"

"Aye, she's here, but I can tell you're hiding something," she said, moving about the meadow to collect her arrows to return them to the quiver. She could sense it in the way she knew things.

What secrets did Derric Corbett hold?

She bent over to retrieve an arrow, glancing back at him—only to catch him staring straight at her arse, his gaze quite pleased with what he saw. She bolted upright.

Something flickered on his face, but he recovered quickly. "I have naught to hide. But I can tell something is wrong. What happened?"

"Naught. Why do you ask?" She bent over again for the next arrow and watched him, not surprised to see his mouth drop open. If a huge pine had been felled next to him, sending a hundred crows into flight, she doubted he'd have noticed.

She stood up and turned to him, a wee smile on her face because now she had something she could use against him.

He knew his lips had a special way of tormenting her. That she couldn't change.

But now she knew he liked her arse.

"You can't fool me, Diamond. You may have an uncanny ability to guess the future, but I have my own special skill."

"You do?" she drawled. "Please do tell. I've been trying to determine if you have any at all."

"My skill is the ability to tell when something is bothering you. And whatever 'tis, I can see 'tis weighing heavily on you. What has you so upset?"

She responded with a loud sigh and said, "Two Scottish sheriffs came to warn us that the English are after Grandsire again."

"Who sent them?" His expression turned serious, his comportment telling her he was as upset by this news as she was, though of course that was impossible.

No one worried about her grandfather the way she did. Mayhap Alasdair had before he'd started a family with Emmalin, but now he was more focused on his wife and children. Her other cousins were no better, both of them newly married, turned daft from marriage, sex, and the possibility of bairns. Nay, it was up to her to guard Alex Grant. She was the only one who could think clearly.

But only if Derric wasn't around to cloud her mind with his hard biceps and long blond locks. She shook her head to clear her thoughts. "Edward's

son, the new king. He's a fool, but we're inclined
to take the threat seriously. Grandsire may not be
safe here anymore. I may have to return to Grant
land with him."

"That would be perfect," he said, a sly grin building on his face.

"Why?" she asked, drawing it out.

"Because I'm headed north. Mayhap you'd like
to travel with me. Edward's son will not let up
and King Robert could use your skills. He needs
to convince a few ornery Scots to support him
instead of this daft new English king."

Her arrows all packed up, she said, "Only if
Grandsire decides to travel that way. I go with him.
Come inside, you can visit with Joya for a few days,
then we'll decide who is going where."

She made it over to her horse and had just settled
her things when she found herself airborne. Landing on her saddle with a huff, she shouted, "I can
mount my own horse, if you please."

"I do not doubt the truth of that statement, but
it would have denied me the chance to touch you."

"I suppose you're going to keep trying that the
whole time you're here?" she asked.

His smirk was answer enough.

Then he also winked, because Derric could
never be satisfied so easily.

She scowled back, but truth be told, she was
looking forward to this visit.

When Derric entered the great hall, Alasdair's

son, John, rushed forward, Coira directly behind him. Her face lit up when she saw Derric. She'd become quite fond of him on the journey to MacLintock land some moons back.

But John wouldn't let her step past him. "I proteck you."

Coira stopped, and John peered up at Derric and asked, "You Engwish?"

Derric ruffled his hair and said, "I'm not English. You remember me, do you not?"

John spat into the bowl at one side of the door, and Coira ran to Derric's side, tugging on his trews. He hoisted her up and settled her on his hip. "Are you happy here, sweet one?"

Coira giggled and nodded. "Lora is here, too, but she's up there." She pointed to the balcony. "And I have someone to play with. He's not mean to me. John likes me."

He felt rather than saw Dyna watching him, but before he could look back, Joya sprung up out of the chair where she'd been sitting near the hearth. "Derric?" she said in disbelief, hurrying over. He set Coira down and hugged his sister, grateful to see her looking so hale.

A quick glance revealed the hall was empty but for Joya and the bairns—Ailith was playing with some fabric animals. The sound of a closing door had him turning around, and he saw Dyna had left. Part of him wanted to go after her, but Joya started leading him over to the hearth. "You are well, sister? Does Els treat you kindly?"

"Aye, he does," she said, sitting down and gesturing for him to do the same. "We're waiting to see where we go next. You came in with Dyna, so I'm sure she told you about the situation with Alex." When he nodded, she leaned forward to whisper. "I can see he's troubled by this. More so than he has been in the past. I don't know what he has planned, but he's conjuring something up."

As if he'd known they were speaking about him, Alex Grant strode into the hall, still walking on his own with nothing for support. It truly was a marvel. Perhaps it was because he lived on the road and on the run, but Derric had never known anyone as old as Alex Grant. Alex approached them directly.

"Greetings to you, Alex," Derric said.

"Corbett. Tell me what news you have for us? Have you seen any garrisons nearby? Any small factions of soldiers near here?" The elder Grant's intense scrutiny sometimes unsettled him, but he answered him as best he could.

"Nay, I've seen no one. I intend to stay here for a few days, assuming no one has any objection"—his sister beamed at him—"then head north to catch up with King Robert eventually. I have a couple of errands to do first."

"So Robert is going north. I'd heard the rumblings, but I'm grateful for a direct account. They say England's new king has run back home. I hope he stays there."

"He still has the coin and the men to order about as he wishes," Derric cautioned. They'd certainly felt the sting of it more than once.

The door burst open, and Joya's husband, Els,

entered the hall with Alasdair. "Corbett," Els called out, "we heard you were here. We're going hunting. Care to join us?"

"Sure. If my sister doesn't mind," he said, glancing over to see her reaction.

"Go," she urged. "I want you to get to know Els better. Go and have fun!"

"May I grab something to eat first? I'm sure you have better offerings than what I've had the last few days." His stomach growled in anticipation of a warm loaf of bread or a fruit pastry.

"Aye," Alasdair said, "we won't be leaving for half an hour. I'll show you where you can sleep so you can settle your things. You're staying awhile, aye?"

"If you'll have me, I'd like to visit with Joya for a few days. Then I'm headed north."

"Follow me," Alasdair said. "Joya can find you something in the kitchens while I show you to your chamber."

Derric followed Alasdair upstairs to a chamber at the end of the passageway. "There are four beds in here, but no one is using it at present. You have it to yourself."

"Many thanks to you. This suits me fine. I enjoy sleeping on a bed once in a while. You know how hard the ground can be."

Derric threw his saddlebag and a few things onto a nearby chest as Alasdair turned to leave. Except he *didn't* leave—he stopped at the door and said, "I hope you aren't here to play with my cousin's feelings."

Perhaps Derric should have expected something

like this, but he hadn't. Alasdair had caught him completely off guard. He set his hands on his hips and asked, "What exactly do you mean by that?"

"I know you like to taunt Dyna, and I see something between the two of you. But remember, she's not some camp follower to be used and tossed aside."

Derric's back bristled at the implication, but he reminded himself that Alasdair had a right to be protective of his cousin. And this was his castle— Derric was relying on his hospitality. "I would never do that to Dyna. I have more respect for her than any lass I've met other than my sister."

"Good, although I do recall you not having much respect for your sister. Either way, you need to respect Dyna or you'll have many to answer to here at MacLintock Castle. Or anywhere. Keep that thought foremost in your head while you're a guest on MacLintock land."

Alasdair gave him one final steel-eyed glance, then left. Bloody hell, but the man seemed to be more like Alexander Grant every time he saw him. Alex could unsettle him with just a look. He didn't wish to have the same with Alasdair.

Derric slumped onto one of the beds, thinking over his words. He was lucky Alasdair had phrased it as a mild threat and not a question. In truth, he wasn't quite sure what his intentions were. Did he need to think about it on MacLintock land with all of Dyna's male cousins around?

He thought of Senga, how she'd been all soft and curvy, always smiling. He'd enjoyed her company, for certes, but he'd never considered marrying her. The only time they'd spent together had been in bed.

Then he thought of Dyna. Diamond was a challenge, but one that invigorated him. Talking to her was almost as much fun as kissing her, and he'd loved every minute he'd spent with her. She was easy to taunt and tease, but he only did it in fun. At first, she'd taken him too seriously, but now she seemed to understand that many of his comments were meant as jests.

She was the one he was drawn to, the one he'd come to see here on MacLintock land. Dyna was the kind of lass he'd marry, not Senga. But did he have a chance with her?

He intended to find out. Before he searched for Senga, he needed to understand this hold Dyna had over him. Why did he go to bed every night with ice blue eyes on his mind? Why did he keep reliving every conversation—and kiss—they'd ever shared? That had to mean something.

But what will you do if the lassie is your daughter?

He didn't think it likely, but it was possible. And if it was true…

He knew the honorable thing to do would be to propose marriage, but could he? Knowing he and Senga didn't suit would make it difficult to commit to marrying her. Especially since he cared so deeply for another woman.

He shook his head, telling himself to slow down. First, he needed to see if he and Dyna suited. Once he knew the answer to that question, then he'd seek out Senga, find out the truth of the wee bairn's parentage.

A knock sounded at his door and he answered. Joya stood outside and said, "I have a meat pie and an ale for you. Elspeth brought some water to freshen up. The others will be leaving shortly, so don't delay."

"My thanks. I'll be right along." He took the small meal and Joya headed back down the stairs. Elspeth left a pitcher and departed as quickly as she'd arrived.

He washed his face and hands from the ewer of water Elspeth had brought, pouring it into a basin and using a linen square he found in the chest by his bed.

Then he left, a little unsettled that he was about to go hunting with the Grant men, all of whom probably felt as Alasdair did, but he reminded himself that he could learn from them. He'd certainly picked up sword skills from fighting with them.

He had to hope Dyna wouldn't go along because she'd be a sheer distraction for him, and all of her cousins would notice.

The shape of her sweet arse was firmly implanted in his mind.

CHAPTER THREE

DERRIC RODE OUT BEHIND ALASDAIR and Els. "My sister says you make her happy, Els. My thanks to you for that."

Els grinned. "We are happy. More than I thought possible. Now if we could put an end to the threat against Grandsire, we'd be able to relax a bit. Help Alasdair build a new tower since he's always having guests."

"And it would be most appreciated," Alasdair said. "We'll hope for a bountiful table this eve. Emmalin already has the loaves of bread baking along with the lamb pies and pear and apple tarts. Just need the boar or a nice deer."

"I like the sound of it," Derric said. "Boar is plentiful here?"

"Boar and pheasant," Els said.

As soon as he finished his sentence, an arrow sluiced over their heads, taking out a bird mid-air, landing not far from them. Dyna flew by them on her horse with a grin on her face. "I have my quarry."

Derric rode behind her to see what she'd felled. He glanced behind him to make sure no one else could hear him. "Nice pheasant, Diamond. Plump breast that will taste sweet, I'm sure."

She said nothing, instead picking up the bird and attaching it to her horse. Then she turned to him with a pointed gaze. "We'll see what *you* catch, Corbett."

With that, she mounted and galloped off, cutting in front of the men. To his surprise, Lora and Joya joined her on their own mounts, followed by five guards.

"Where are you lasses headed?" Els asked.

Joya smiled sweetly and said, "We're off to the loch. Our mission is waterfowl. You men go off for your boar and mayhap a wee rabbit or two."

Els snorted. "You don't know your husband well if you think a rabbit's leg will satisfy my needs this eve. I've a huge appetite." His voice carried across the glen, and his wife's laughter trailed back.

"And don't I know it," she shouted back.

Alex had ridden out from the keep too, although Derric hadn't noticed until now. His horse was drawn up next to Alasdair's, and the two were talking quietly. But Alex broke away and nodded to his other grandsons. "I'll go with the lasses for now," he said. "I'll come looking for you once they head back. 'Tis a beautiful autumn day and I plan to enjoy it."

Els said, "Aye, Joya won't be out here more than an hour. She's just along for the ride."

"With Dyna shooting, they may only need half

an hour," Alasdair said. "I hear Lora's archery skills are improving, too."

Alex nodded again and rode off after the lasses, and Alasdair led their small hunting group into the woods.

"Are we more likely to find boar or deer?" Derric asked Els as they moved along.

"We often see deer, but they're too fast to hit on horseback. We have better luck with boar in these woods. They're plentiful, though sometimes an arrow in a boar's flank will only slow it instead of killing it. If we find one, we may have to stop and finish it with our sword."

Derric listened with interest. He did like to eat well, and since he spent much of his time camping, he would be wise to learn their hunting strategies. Although he'd attempted to master a bow in the hopes of catching some meat to fatten up their daily meals, he wasn't nearly as skilled as any of the Grants. Perhaps he'd ask Dyna to work with him.

Aye, he thought, imagining what it would be like to stand with her, their bodies pressed together, while she helped him aim an arrow at a target—*that would be quite nice*. But he knew it unwise to dwell on such thoughts in his present company. Her cousins certainly wouldn't approve of his musings.

Would they approve of him as a husband for Dyna? Perhaps he'd pose the question to Joya, see what she thought.

They traveled through the cool morn, gray skies above them but no rain yet. Once they settled into silence, the sounds of the forest started to reemerge. The squirrels were still busy searching for nuts to store for winter, and the sound of leaves falling from the trees whenever a gust of wind broke through was a constant reminder that cold weather was on its way.

Els held his hand up, stopping the group. They all quieted, their right hands reaching for their bows. Derek watched, his dagger in hand. Two of the horses became skittish, indicating there was some creature hiding in the nearby bushes.

A snort alerted them to the presence of wild pigs not far ahead of them. They moved their horses apart, waiting for one to come into their view.

Derric whispered, "Don't they travel in a herd? Are you not worried they'll attack us?" He'd seen them in the wild many times, and he'd always stayed away. Many Scots had been gored by the beasts' tusks, their weight such that they were easily able to overpower a man. He preferred lamb or beef.

"Nay," Els said. "They'll run the other way most of the time. Only if they feel threatened will they retaliate."

Just then, a squealing boar came out of the bushes, not far from Alasdair, and gave him his broad side. Els and Alasdair both fired, striking the wild animal twice in its flank. It squealed and started to run clumsily around the area.

Alasdair glanced at Els and said, "We have to finish it."

The two dismounted and raced after the injured

animal. Els motioned to Derric and said, "Follow us. We may need your help."

Although he couldn't think why they'd need three men to take down a boar, they were more experienced hunters, so he jumped off his horse and followed.

They managed to herd the animal in a clearing, its movements slowing from the injuries.

Alasdair shouted over his shoulder, "Derric, you want to finish him?"

Derric arched his brow at the suggestion. "Your kill. You have the honors. I can't believe you caught one this fast."

Els spoke quietly to Alasdair, then they moved in on the boar, coming at it from opposite sides. One made a signal, and then they both raced at the beast, catching it and tossing it down on its side.

It took two of them to hold the beast down. Alasdair had to speak in intervals from the exertion of holding the fighting animal in place, but his message was clear. "Shall we let it go and send it your way, Corbett?"

Derric backed up. "Hell, nay. I've never caught a boar before. You have him. Why send him to me?" He'd always been good with animals, but the animals he dealt with were tamed beasts. Horses. Dogs. He had no experience with wild pigs. Nor did he want any.

"You look a wee bit green, Corbett." Els tipped his head and smirked. "Remember this moment, because if you mistreat Dyna, we'll find another animal just like this and send it after you."

Alasdair added, "We all know you have a special talent with horses. Shall we see if it extends to wild pigs? If we let him loose, will he come over for a sweet nuzzle?" His expression was dead serious.

"What?" Derric couldn't believe what he'd just heard. Dyna's cousins had just threatened him with bodily harm because he was interested in her.

Alasdair gave the beast a quick death, then brought his serious gaze back to Derric, giving him a look that would make a lusty whore run in the other direction. "Do anything to Dyna that we deem unacceptable or she doesn't like, and we *will* make certain you suffer for it. Understand?"

Derric gulped, his voice coming out barely audible. "Aye."

"I couldn't hear you."

"Aye, I'll not hurt your cousin. Not intentionally."

"What the hell does that mean?" Alasdair left the dead animal and stalked across the clearing toward Derric. "Are you challenging me?"

Derric didn't know how to deflate this situation, but he knew better than to anger Dyna's powerful cousins when he had no friends to assist him. "I meant no disrespect. It would never be my intention for her to get hurt. Emotionally or physically."

They both nodded, apparently accepting his response. The boar was a large animal, which hopefully meant they'd be heading back to the castle soon. He wasn't sure how much more "hunting" he could take.

The distant sound of hoofbeats met his ears,

becoming louder, and Alex rode into the clearing on his horse and drew up close to Derric. "Join me in a canter while they clean up our dinner?"

With a sigh of relief and a nod, he tried not to move too quickly toward his horse. He would be grateful for some distance from Dyna's cousins just now. It hadn't been a pleasant conversation.

They rode quietly for several minutes before Alex slowed his mount and Derric did the same.

"They love their cousin," Alex said, "but don't expect their disapproval to be as harsh as they suggest. If the two of you don't suit, then you move on, but only after being honest with my granddaughter. You need to spend time together to see if you suit."

"I agree, and many thanks to you, my lord." He wiped his hand down his sweaty face. "'Tis a fine stallion you ride."

"I've had several dependable warhorses, all descendants of my first one, Midnight."

"What do you call this one?"

"Midnight," Alex said, his mouth tipping up slightly. "He's earned it."

Derric noticed the man rode like he had a special connection with his horse, something he admired. The relationship between a horse and its rider was a sacred thing. Derric had developed a talent with horses years ago when he'd first joined William Wallace. Being one of the new men, he hadn't possessed his own horse—but he'd soon learned that there were horses to be acquired in any battle…if you could get them to stay with you. Soft words and a pat or two did far more than whipping an animal. He'd noticed that the Grant mounts never bore any scars on their flesh. A pheasant flew within the beast's vision, and the horse didn't respond at all. Derric's horse nearly bolted, and the rabbit that ran across their path spooked him even more. He leaned down to calm the horse with soft words, stroking its neck. This horse was one from the MacLintock stables, assigned to him because his horse was still weary from the ride.

Midnight didn't wiggle an ear.

"He's finely trained, my lord. How do you do it?"

True, he knew quite a bit about taming horses, but Alex Grant had to be well into his seventies. He'd trained more horses than Derric by far.

"I treat him well. The secret to most everything in this life. He gets plenty of exercise and fine food, and he's always rewarded for difficult journeys. I train with him often. Do you know my wife used to sneak out to feed my first warhorse apples whenever he brought me home safely from battle? She thought I didn't know, but I could tell just by the way he always nudged her, his muzzle targeting the pockets she used to sew in her gowns."

"Didn't the horse hold more loyalty to her?"

"Nay, he sensed my relationship with her. Now back to that other issue."

"Issue?" Derric had no idea any issue had been raised.

"Treat others well. I'm pleased you have an interest in my granddaughter, but I must act in my son's place since he is not here. What are your intentions with Dyna?"

Derric had to catch himself from falling off his horse. Alex glanced over and arched a brow at him. Swallowing hard, he decided honesty was the best approach. He doubted he could fool someone so wise and experienced. "'Struth is I'm unsure. I like Dyna, but with the war going on, we haven't had enough of a chance to see if we suit. I'd like to find out. I came to visit Joya, but I also wished to spend more time with Dyna. She's a fine lass, my lord. But I don't know if she has any interest in me or in marriage."

"You're willing to offer marriage?"

"I would like to explore the possibility." Derric cleared his throat. He hadn't expected such direct questions, although he respected the man for being clear.

Unlike Els and Alasdair.

"Where do you go from here? And where is your permanent home?"

"I don't have a permanent home. Ever since my parents were killed, I've traveled the land of the Scots to fight for our freedom, first with William Wallace and now with King Robert. The forest is my home. I quite enjoy a cooked meal and a soft bed on occasion."

"Feel free to offer for her, or discuss the possibility with Dyna, but make sure my granddaughter isn't in that soft bed unless you've said your vows. Our clan accepts handfasting, so do not think to get her with child without handfasting first." The man kept his eyes straight ahead, Derric blushing with sweat dripping out of his pores. He'd never dealt with the father of a love interest.

He'd never had another love interest.

The man wasn't going to leave him be. Perhaps fighting the boar might have been easier.

He supposed he needed to make a comment about that statement, so he mumbled, "Understood."

"What is it that draws you to my granddaughter?"

Her arse probably wasn't the best answer, though it was his first thought. But Dyna had many other fine qualities. "Many reasons, if I'm truthful with you. I enjoy bantering with her—she has a biting sense of humor that I quite enjoy. Of course you know she's a beautiful woman, and she's fierce and highly skilled with her bow." He hoped he'd given enough reasons. He couldn't think of any others at the moment. Gripping the reins was becoming a challenge so he alternated hands, wiping the sweat from his palms onto his trews.

Alex's next statement served as a warning. He could tell in the way he held his profile. "You will be kind to her soft heart. Do not do anything to damage it or change her. If you will promise me that much, you have my blessing to pursue her. I don't worry about your travels. She would prefer to wander the Highlands, I think, as if she's honor bound to protect the land herself. I cannot stop her from traveling, but I trust you to treat her with respect and guard her soft heart. That much I must insist on."

"Her soft heart?" Derric was so stunned by those words, words he'd never tied to the lass, that he wasn't sure how to react. "I've never seen any evidence of a soft heart. She's a hardened warrior, no disrespect intended, my lord."

Alex Grant stopped his horse and turned him to face Derric. "I suppose I could understand that comment since you've only been around her during verra trying times, but my instinct is to send you away for that. Dyna has the softest heart of any of my grandbairns. If you haven't taken the time or invested the effort to see that truth, then you don't deserve the honor of courting her. You have a short time to see if you can meet that quest, but if you still believe your statement after that, I'll send you off MacLintock land."

In that case, it was a good thing he hadn't told the patriarch the reasoning behind his pet name for Dyna. While he'd seen glimpses of Dyna's soft heart in the spring—what hard-hearted woman would set out to rescue a bairn?—but she'd been so full of rage toward the lassie's uncaring father that it had eclipsed any show of warmth.

Alex turned his horse around and headed back toward their original location, stirring up a cloud of dust in his direction.

The wizened warrior had challenged him to a quest that he had no idea how to accomplish. How did one find out about a lass's heart?

He may have escaped being attacked by a wild hog, but he felt like he'd just been strung up by his bollocks.

CHAPTER FOUR

DYNA, JOYA, AND LORA PROUDLY returned to the keep, bearing their gifts for the eve's feast. Grandsire had stayed out with the lads, simply because he loved horseback riding and the chance to be outside the gates. The two pheasants and two ducks they'd brought down would feed many.

They rode through the courtyard, to a couple rounds of applause at the sight of their catch, then left their horses in the stables and headed into the kitchens with their bounty. After they handed the game off to the smiling cook, Dyna washed up in her chamber and then returned to the great hall, finding it mostly empty except for Joya and Emmalin and the bairns. It was exactly as she'd hoped.

"You did a fine job," Emmalin said as she fiddled with the needlework on her lap. "Alasdair and I love pheasant. My thanks for taking two down."

Being bold had always been Dyna's favored approach, and she had no reason to believe the current occasion should be any different. "Do you mind if I ask you two some personal questions?"

She did her best to ignore the sudden flip-flops in her belly.

Joya said, "Of course, ask anything you'd like." She gave a quick glance to Emmalin, probably because they had no idea what she was about to say.

Dyna forged onward, ignoring the sudden sweat on her palms. "What think you of the marriage bed?"

Joya spat out her drink and laughed, while Emmalin dropped her needle into her lap and stared up at Dyna, the expression on her face one of sheer shock.

Well, she had been blunt about it. She gritted her teeth because her instinct was to suggest they should forget she'd asked, but she *had* wondered about this. Quite a bit, in fact. And now that Derric had become so appealing to her, she needed an answer.

Neither Joya nor Emmalin said a word, making her quite uncomfortable, so she explained, "I would like to know if you are pleased with it. I hear it hurts the first time and I'm just curious."

Joya looked at Emmalin and said, "You'll have to explain about the first time. Mine was not one I care to remember."

Emmalin and Dyna both knew the reason for that—Joya had been kidnapped and raped after she ran away from her aunt's home—so Emmalin was quick to nod. "As you wish." Then set her needle-work aside and gave Dyna her full attention. "The first time hurts, but not badly. And it doesn't hurt for long. You know how it happens, do you not? Many think 'tis like animals, but we do it mostly face to face."

"I understand. Mama explained it to me and I've listened to plenty of serving lasses and maids talk about their exploits with their husbands. But I wanted to talk about this with someone I trust. Like a pinch?"

Emmalin thought for a moment, then continued, "I'll be honest. It was more than a pinch for me. Aye, it hurt, but it did not hurt for long."

Joya interjected with a grin, "And the pleasure you gain makes it worthwhile. I cannot get enough of Els."

"My first husband was only interested in his own pleasure. 'Tis an entirely different experience with Alasdair, thank goodness." Emmalin blushed, dropping the volume of her voice. "'Struth is, in the beginning, I wished to do it more than he did… and he wished to do it often enough." She looked up at Dyna and said, "You need to make sure you choose the right man. 'Tis wonderful when you suit. If you love the other person, you worry about their pleasure as much as your own."

"Pleasure?" she asked, pressing them for more.

Joya was nearly as blunt as Dyna. "'Tis called an orgasm. Your husband must help you get there, but once you do, I swear a castle could crumble around me and I'd never know it. On one occasion a thunderstorm was ripping through the night, and Els thought it was his climax."

"Poor Ailith was crying one night and I never

heard her." Emmalin giggled into her hand.

Joya glanced over her shoulder for anyone within hearing distance—the bairns were playing at the far end of the hall, not within hearing—before she continued. She leaned forward and lowered her voice. "We were in the woods once and didn't hear the snort of a boar until 'twas almost upon us. I'll always remember the image of Els using his sword with his bollocks hanging out. He only had to wound the beast before it took off."

Emmalin gave a bark of laughter and stomped her foot on the floor in glee. "Did you finish?"

"Hell, nay. I told him to put it away," Joya said, her brow furrowed. "The big snout on the boar finished it for me. It was so ugly."

"John heard us one night and ran into our chamber. He asked Alasdair why he was hugging me so hard and shouting," Emmalin said, her eyes wide.

The two started laughed hysterically, and it went on for so long that Dyna eventually couldn't help but join them.

She didn't know what to make of their revelations, except she had a sudden desire to understand exactly what they meant. Which meant she needed a man. Taking advantage of their situation, she posed one more question. "My mama told me a woman's maidenhead is naught more than a piece of skin covering an opening. Why are lasses forced to wait to do the act when men aren't expected to do the same?"

The laughter stopped immediately, and Joya stared at Emmalin. "I don't know."

Emmalin concurred. "I don't know either. I think a man wants a woman who has never been touched by another."

"Then can't a woman want a man who's never been touched?"

Emmalin blurted out, "If that were the case, no one would know how to do it. A husband teaches a wife. Imagine trying to figure it out on your own on your wedding night." That caused Joya and Emmalin to burst into a fresh round of laughter, but the door opened and the men returned, putting an end to their antics.

The feast began early once Alexander Grant announced he had decided to leave for Cameron land on the morrow. At first everyone was somber at the news, but Emmalin found a couple of minstrels to attend and the festivities became lively and joyful.

Derric sat at a trestle table with Joya and Els, a few Grant guards he didn't know, and Dyna. He hadn't had the chance to speak with her much since his arrival, but his desire for her hadn't abated one bit.

Even if it did make him wonder if he was going to get strung up by the bollocks or attacked by a wild boar.

The pressure was on him to make a decision. He either had to approach Dyna about her feelings or leave her behind and go on his way.

He certainly didn't intend to just leave, yet he

didn't know how to pursue her with all of her male kin watching his every move. He'd never been in a situation like this before.

Alex sat at the dais with Emmalin, Alasdair, and the wee ones, John sitting next to *Seanair*. Four other long tables bustled with other clan members.

The hall had a joyous atmosphere, just as it had on Derric's other visits to MacLintock land, and he felt a pit of emptiness inside of him. He'd been constantly on the move ever since his parents had been killed. It was a hard life, but one he liked. Or so he'd always told himself. But now, sitting with this clan, experiencing their warmth for one another—even if the men currently didn't have much warmth for him—made him question everything he'd thought he knew.

King Robert had asked him once what he wanted out of his life. He wanted to arrive at the gates of heaven and have his parents greet him with smiles on their faces instead of what he knew would happen: his mother would be crying and his father would be comforting her. They'd be grief-stricken for all Joya had experienced. For the way Derric had left her alone.

He hadn't attempted to explain this to Robert, instead telling him he wished to see Scotland free. It was the only answer he could think of that drew him away from the guilt that riddled him every day. The decision to leave had been easier when he'd thought he was doing what was best for Joya, when he hadn't known it had almost killed her.

He glanced over at her, Joya's happiness showing in her face, her voice, her laughter. One would think his guilt would have eased now that she'd found such happiness with her husband, but it hadn't.

Probably because he'd only just learned about the reivers who had attacked and raped her years before. He couldn't stop thinking about it. He couldn't stop stewing in the guilt.

How he wished they'd had the childhood of a Grant instead of losing their parents so young.

He tried to shake the dark thoughts away, wanting to enjoy the food, the company, and the revelry. This would be a night to remember, he was sure of it.

The group hadn't been seated long when the serving lasses brought out platters of food. The smell of roasted pheasant caught Derric first. None of them he traveled with could shoot a pheasant down. His diet consisted mostly of rabbit and duck, though he caught an occasional fish or two to roast and enjoy. Alasdair had cut a huge piece of the wild pig so they could savor some at the feast tonight. The rest would be roasted overnight on the spit.

A platter of sliced pig meat was set on their table, and his mouth watered at the sight of it. The dishes kept coming: two crusty loaves of dark bread; a bowl of baked apples and pears dotted with cinnamon; mutton meat pies; bowls of cabbage; and a mix of carrots, parsnips, and peas.

Joya said, "Brother, close your mouth before the drool shows."

Els laughed. "The poor lad is starving. He's been

eating camp food mostly. Who can blame him? Other than an occasional pigeon and lots of rabbit, he gets no meat to eat."

"Laugh as you will, but I've been able to catch a few fish of late. But this all looks delicious. I will indeed enjoy it. Especially the pheasant." He winked at Dyna.

She just shot him a look and reached for the bowl of vegetables. He cast a few furtive glances at her as he served himself—seeing her take a hunk of bread and then try her first bite of the apple and pear concoction. She closed her eyes and licked her lips, sighing deeply.

Derric dropped his utensil on the table at the sweet sound coming from the lass.

Joya elbowed Els, but Derric never said anything, instead returning to his food. Still entranced with all the offerings, the only thing that had interrupted his thoughts had been Dyna's nearly carnal moaning.

Joya asked, "So have you decided where you're going next, brother dear?"

In between chews and a quick sip of mead, Derric mumbled, "North."

She didn't ask any more, instead turning to Dyna. "And what about you?"

"I'll travel with Grandsire, make sure he arrives at Cameron land without any mishaps. I'd be lying if I said I wasn't worried about another fool coming out of the woods and capturing him. I won't rest until he arrives there safely. After that, I'll head to Grant land, see my parents and my sisters and brothers."

"How has Claray been through all of the trouble with Grandsire?" Els wrapped his arm around his wife, squeezing her shoulders while he waited for Dyna's reply.

"Not the best. I need to see her. She's always calmer when I'm around. Sometimes I feel guilty about leaving."

Joya chewed on a meat pie, staring up at the beams in the ceiling thoughtfully. "Do I know Claray? I've not heard of her."

"Aye, I think I told you about her when we were in Glasgow or Ayr, though I probably did not give you her name. She's my half-sister. She was three when my parents married. My father found my mother in an awful situation where some bad men were forcing her to do their bidding by holding wee Claray captive. It had a long-lasting effect on both of them. They still suffer nightmares." She glanced at Derric before looking back at Joya. "In fact, Claray is still so troubled that I feel guilty every time I leave home. The nightmares are relentless, and she depends on me to rescue her from the evil she senses around her."

"Evil?" Joya asked.

"Spiders, mostly," Els blurted that out and then gave Dyna an apologetic look.

"Spiders?" Derric had heard of odd nightmares, but this was unusual.

Why would they dream of spiders?

Dyna gave him a look that told him not to ask, so he closed his mouth. "You can explain it to me some other time."

"Thank you," Dyna said. "Claray is four years older than I am, but she's still child-like in many ways."

"'Tis quite sad, Dyna," Joya said. "Forgive me for prying."

"You'll meet her someday, Joya. 'Tis good to know ahead of time." Dyna stood up from the table, finished with her meal. "I think I'll go for a stroll. I love the night sky and 'tis especially clear this eve."

"May I join you?" Derric asked quickly, clearly surprising everyone. Els cast a hard look his way. Were he not in the MacLintock great hall, he would have shouted at him that he wasn't about to attack his cousin. Instead, he kept his silence, waiting for her response.

Dyna nodded, so he left his place and headed out the door with her.

His only question was, how did one go about asking a woman if she was interested in a relationship?

If only he was as good with women as he was with horses.

CHAPTER FIVE

DYNA DID HER BEST TO calm the fluttering in her belly. She hadn't expected Derric to volunteer to come along, especially after watching him down so much food. "I'm surprised you can move at all after the amount you ate."

He chuckled. "'Twas hard to walk away, but 'tis for the best. I haven't eaten a meal like that in a long time. The cinnamon flavoring in the apples is quite unique. I've never tried it before." He paused for a moment, his expression turning serious. "I'm sorry about your sister, but I'd like to meet her sometime."

"She'd be hesitant to meet you. It takes her a long time to trust people. Especially men."

"How do you remember all your aunts, uncles, and cousins? You have so many."

"They're each special in their own way." Whenever she thought about them all, she couldn't help but smile. She knew she'd been blessed many times over by being born a Grant. "There are so many older relatives who've watched over and guided me that I can't imagine how it was for you and Joya after you lost your parents."

Derric chewed on his lip and nodded. "Aye. When I look back on it, I can't believe I was so hasty to leave Joya with our aunt. I think I was in shock." They meandered through the courtyard, taking their time, something unlike both of them. The sky was surprisingly bright, no clouds in sight.

She glanced over at him, surprised to see such a vulnerable side of him. "With both of your parents dead, where else could you have left her? You did the best thing you could have done. Your aunt may not have been warm toward her, but she didn't harm her. The marauders who hurt her found her long after you had left. That had naught to do with you." It had become clear to her that he blamed himself for what had happened, and that the weight of it wore on him. "You did what you had to do to survive—and to see that she did too."

"Mayhap you are right. Unfortunately, our auntie was not as loving as many of yours seem to be. Do you have a favorite? Nay, I think I can guess. Your aunt who is the skilled archer."

"Aunt Gwyneth is not truly my aunt, but she and two of her daughters are the renowned archers in the family. The only way I'm related to the Ramsays is because my aunt married the old laird. But we've been so close to the Ramsays that I call them all aunts and uncles." She smiled, warmed by the thought of her family. "So I have many aunts and uncles, all special in their way. But I also have many great aunts and uncles, though I've lost some. We lost Uncle Jake and Aunt Aline several years ago, and it's been difficult for Alasdair, especially since he has no siblings. Uncle Jamie and Aunt Gracie are kind and strong, and such good listeners. They always help me when I'm troubled. Aunt Kyla and Uncle Finlay are much more outgoing and they always speak their minds. Aunt Kyla loves to plan festivals and will do anything for Grandsire. Aunt Maeve is sweet as can be.

"My great aunt and uncles are much more colorful because they live in so many different places. I love traveling to visit with each of them, and we're always welcome. Aunt Avelina is a seer, and a couple of cousins also have the same ability. Aunt Diana is the laird of the Drummond clan. She spoils all of her nieces because she only has boys. Aunt Celestina and Uncle Brodie adopted an orphan." She pointed to a bench in the garden where they could sit.

"How did that come to be?"

"Uncle Brodie found Loki living behind a tavern. He used a crate to protect himself in bad weather. They say he was a cheeky lad, cunning and bold. Once he grew, he was a fine fighter, almost better with a sword than Grandsire and Papa. Then there's Uncle Robbie and Aunt Caralyn, who taught us how to swim and fish, though Uncle Robbie has passed on. I have so many special family members. I wish you could meet them all."

"It must be a challenge to remember them all. 'Twould be a treat for me to have even a couple to visit, especially the strongest warriors. So you have no favorites?"

"Aye, I suppose I do," she said with a smile. "I think my favorites would have to be Aunt Jennie and Uncle Aedan, even though I don't see them nearly enough. I'm glad that Grandsire wants to go to Cameron land, truly. It'll be wonderful to see them again."

"What makes them so special?"

She pointed at the night sky. "They know the stars." She grabbed his hand, his eyes glimmering at her touch, and tugged him. "Here, I'll show you. 'Tis a perfect night." They went out through the gates, waving to one of the guards, which meant they were to watch over her. "Just to the hill," she said, pointing. Then she whispered to Derric, "If I go far, I must take five guards with me. If they can see me, they'll let us go alone."

She tugged on his hand and ran to the hill, letting go when they started climbing. They exchanged a look and started hurtling up as fast as they could, racing, their laughter echoing across the meadow. Derric was ahead of her for a time, but he'd started too fast and finished slow. Dyna shook her head as she pushed past him and reached the summit, a flat area in the middle with no trees and soft grass. "Too slow. Keep eating all that food."

She stood there for a moment, soaking in the view, then turned to him. "Lie down next to me." Without waiting to see if he'd join her, she lay on her back and stared up at the sky. The clear night was full of sparkling stars, twinkling in all their glory.

"Like hell," he said, his hands on his hips. "The guards can see us, and I've been warned and threatened by both your grandsire and your overprotective cousins."

"Pay them no mind. Look up," she said, although she wasn't surprised to see her family had been blustering. They couldn't seem to understand that she could take care of herself. "See what you're missing. We'll not even touch, if that pleases you." She knew he'd be surprised by the view. Even though the men who traveled with the Bruce slept under the stars, it was often under cover of pines in case it rained, and the sky was rarely this clear. Scotland was often cloudy.

And it was a glorious sight to see this eve.

He didn't rush to join her, glancing back at the guards.

She arched a brow at him. "My cousins scared you?"

"Nay," he said, quickly settling himself on his back next to her and looking up at the stars.

They lay like that for a long time, side by side, staring up at the sky, then he finally broke the silence with a whistle. "I've seen stars at night, but none this bright. Why?"

"'Tis a clear night. No clouds. Uncle Aedan and Aunt Jennie invited us to sleep outside with them one night at the top of their large flat hill. I'll show you what they taught me." She pointed to one area of the sky. "The stars are arranged the same every night and 'tis fun to pick out their shapes."

"Where?"

"I'll help you get started. Do you not see the shape like a ladle over there?" She pointed off to the side.

"I do. And there's a smaller one like it nearby, is there not?"

"Aye! Good. You found it quickly."

They continued on, pointing out what they saw, laughing and enjoying each other's company. They found various shapes and animals in addition to what Aunt Jennie had shown Dyna. At one point, she turned her head and found Derric staring at her. "What's wrong?"

"Naught. I'm enjoying watching you. I've not seen you laugh like this before."

She blushed, accepting that what he said was probably true. She carried much worry in her life, not for herself, but for her sister, her mother, and her grandsire. What was more, she'd learned long ago that men rarely took a smiling woman seriously. They were too busy looking for a soft mound of hay to lay her against. She'd crafted her serious look over a matter of months, testing and learning which one kept men away the most. Her mother had helped her with it because she'd experienced the same thing. Sela Seton had become so adept at keeping men at a distance she'd earned herself the title of "Ice Queen."

"'Tis a cover, Derric. It keeps me safe from men I don't want near me."

"And will you allow this one closer?"

"Aye," she whispered, turning toward him.

He leaned toward her, cupped her cheek, and

settled his lips on hers in a softer kiss than she'd expected. His tongue pressed at the seam of her lips and she parted for him, allowing him inside. He tasted of apples and cinnamon. She leaned into him, wanting more, as his mouth angled over hers in a gentle exploration, teasing and taunting her with the touch of his tongue.

The more he kissed her, the more she wanted. Her nipples peaked, begging to be let out of the confinement of her tunic. The swell of her breasts from just the touch of his lips made her wonder exactly what she was missing.

Derric leaned closer, rolling her onto her back and pressing his upper body against hers. "Dyna, you are so beautiful." He kissed a trail down her neck, pausing to nibble on her ear lobe, the sensation sending shock waves through her body that all seemed to land in the same spot. His hands cupped her breasts through the rough wool of her tunic, and even that caused her body to respond in ways she didn't comprehend. Derric Corbett had a rare ability to put every part of her body into a super-sensitive state that left her wanting more.

How did he do it?

"Derric, stop, please," she said, panting.

He pulled back quickly, a confused look on his face. "Did I do something wrong? I thought you were enjoying this as much as I was." He did his best to straighten a few of her hairs that had gone astray, tucking them behind her ear.

Every place he touched reacted to him. She ran her finger down the rough stubble on his jaw-line, over his full bottom lip. "I do enjoy it. More than you know." His golden locks looked brown at night, gently curling at the ends where they hit his shoulders. "I have a favor to ask of you, Derric. Something unusual. Something I wouldn't ask of anyone else."

"I'll do anything for you if I can."

"All right," she said, pausing to consider what she was planning, wanting to be sure. "But what I want cannot happen here or this eve. We'll have to plan another time."

He looked at her, more confused than ever.

"Take my maidenhead. I don't want it anymore."

CHAPTER SIX

"WHAT THE HELL?" DERRIC JUMPED up as fast as if he'd been struck by ten arrows from a row of Englishmen. He'd never been so shocked over anything another person had said.

She sprung up nearly as quickly. "Not now. I'm just asking if we could arrange for it to happen later."

"Nay." His answer came out in nearly a shout, but he had to fight to control the emotions raging through him. Desire was first and foremost, and it was a nearly painful challenge to tamp it down now that he knew she wanted him. If he'd stayed next to her on that hilltop, it would have been all over in a matter of minutes since she was willing to allow him liberties. She was too bloody tempting.

He couldn't allow that to happen.

He couldn't forget that they were on MacLintock land with two of her cousins and her grandsire, all of whom had threatened to unman him if he did anything disrespectful to the lass. He couldn't forget that the guards were watching them at this moment.

Somehow he didn't think looking at her grand-father and saying, "She wanted me to do it," would suffice.

Els and Alasdair would string him up by his bollocks for all to see. Or...

Visions of her grandsire tying a rope to his bollocks and dragging him behind his horse caused him to sweat, in more places than he'd ever sweat before.

He coughed and began pacing, taunted by the imagery in his mind, which completely reversed his arousal.

"Derric? Am I truly that undesirable to you?"

"What?" He raced over to stand in front of her, taking her hands. "Nay. You're the most beautiful lass I've ever known. And you're courageous and funny. I love talking with you, but..." Bloody hell, but the pain in her gaze made him wish to do what she asked, just to make that look go away.

"But what?"

"I did tell you that your cousins and your grandfather threatened me, did I not? Have you forgotten so quickly? I surely haven't." He began to pace again, running his hands through his hair. Now that he thought on it, he shouldn't be up here with her, or even alone with her. Would the guards tell Alasdair?

What the hell had he been thinking to kiss her the way he had on MacLintock land?

The answer was simple: he had no control over his base urges when it came to Dyna Grant. None.

"But 'tis not their decision. 'Tis mine."

He stopped to stare at her, his hands on his hips. "I doubt they would agree with you, Dyna. You don't really think they would, do you?" He reached for her hand. "Come, we must return, or they'll be coming after me soon."

She followed him for a few paces, then tugged on his hand to stop him. "Derric, wait."

They stood a hand's length apart. She took his chin and forced him to gaze into her eyes. Her beautiful blue eyes were full of hurt, and he hated himself for it. "Lass, I didn't mean to hurt you. Aye, it should be your decision, but you're not a camp follower. You have a clan who watches over you. Have you forgotten you're of noble blood? Even the King of England watches over you just because you're the daughter of a chieftain. He could order your marriage just as he did Emmalin's match with the baron. If I took your maidenhead, I would have to marry you. Are you ready for that?"

Her scowl was so deep that he stepped back and arched his brow. It was a battle of the wrinkling foreheads before either of them said anything.

"What? You wouldn't want to marry me?" he asked, a little hurt by her reaction.

"You would?" The look on her face was so nuanced, he couldn't hope to read it.

Hellfire, but he could feel his own forehead doing things he hadn't told it to do. "If I took your maidenhead, I would want to marry you."

"But 'tis the only reason?"

"Lass, stop forcing me to make decisions about

something that hasn't happened." This was not going well, and he had no idea how to change that. Everything he said seemed to dig the hole he was in a little bit deeper. Soon he'd be burying himself.

"Never mind. I have my answer." She raced ahead of him.

Shite. She was so fast, he couldn't hope to keep up.

Not that he'd know what to say if he managed to catch up. He sure as hell hadn't done anything to complete his quest to find out why her grandsire considered her soft-hearted. A hard arse and a stubborn wench were the terms that came to mind after this interlude.

Nay, that wasn't quite true—he'd seen the flash of pain in her eyes—and yet, he wasn't sure where that left them. He'd hoped to see if they suited, but neither of them seemed able or willing to admit to having strong feelings for the other. The truth was she'd scowled the moment he mentioned marriage.

Mayhap she wasn't interested in anything but a means to an end.

The end of her maidenhead.

Dyna threw the keep door open with a bang, a move she instantly regretted because it brought all the eyes in the hall straight to her.

Every single person in the great hall stared at her, a mass of questioning glances that she had no wish to acknowledge.

Blushing, she nodded, trying not to act flustered

as she made her way up the stairs to her bedchamber. She didn't wish to cause Derric any trouble. Everything they'd done had been her idea. Except for the kiss.

Tears pricked her eyes, and she struggled to hold them back as she entered her chamber and lowered onto the edge of one of the beds. It was a chamber for guests, equipped with enough beds for a few lasses.

Someone knocked on her door a few moments later.

"Enter." She swiped at any tears that had managed to fall, too proud to let on what had happened.

The door opened, revealing Alasdair. He stared at her before he spoke, his usual tactic—assess the situation first, then speak. Hardly her philosophy, but this was her beloved Alasdair.

His chin lifted a bit as he perused her face. "Answer me one question. Was he inappropriate with you?"

"Who?" Doing her best to summon a look of innocence, she glanced up at her cousin from her perch on the bed, not wanting to let on that her problem was indeed related to Derric.

"I think you know," he said, stepping inside. Emmalin came in behind him, but she stayed back to let them talk. "Don't play innocent. He left with you."

"Alasdair, naught happened. Derric did not hurt me." She paused, considering, then said, "But I would ask a question of you."

"I'm listening," he said, moving closer.

She glanced from him to Emmalin and back. "How did you know Emmalin was the right one for you? How did you…When did you… I don't even know exactly what to ask, dammit." Her hands curled around the covers, yanking them sideways. "What made you decide to marry Emmalin?"

Alasdair smiled, something she didn't see often enough. If only it weren't at her expense. "Are you laughing at me?"

"Nay," he said, sitting next to her on the bed. "You just made me think of a conversation I had with Grandsire on the parapets. I asked him how he knew Grandmama was the right one for him."

"And?"

"His answer didn't help. He said he knew when he first saw her, but that he fought against it. In the beginning, he was more concerned about protecting her than anything else. That was how I felt with Emmalin at first. I had a fierce need to protect her, to keep her by my side." He glanced back at Emmalin and reached for her hand. She stepped closer and rested her head on his shoulder. Then he continued, "And you helped me, too, Dyna. Don't you recall yelling at me outside the gates?"

Dyna had forgotten that time, when she'd known he carried so much pain after losing his parents that he couldn't speak of it. That his pain blocked his ability to see Emmalin and the possibility of a relationship with her. "I'd forgotten. That helped you know she was for you?"

"Oddly, aye. I couldn't imagine marrying someone without my parents present, but that was impossible. I had to accept that first. Once I did that, then I could consider marriage. But I never seriously considered standing in front of a priest until I spoke with Grandsire. And after what happened to my da after Mama died...well, I still was unsure. Do you love Derric?"

"I don't know." She paused. "I'm not sure I know what love is. How can I tell?"

"I'll tell you how. When you're in love with someone, you can't bear to be parted from them. When I left Emmalin to return to Grant Castle, all I could think of was returning to MacLintock land. Do you wish to go with Derric when he leaves?"

She gave it some thought, then shrugged. "Sometimes."

"But you'll leave with Grandsire even if Derric chooses not to go with you?"

"Of course. I have to go with Grandsire."

"Then you're not ready for marriage. You're holding back." He gave her an assessing look. "Are you sure he didn't do or say something inappropriate?"

She shook her head. "Nay, but I can take care of myself."

He stepped away from Emmalin, kissing her cheek, then knelt down in front of Dyna. "If anything changes, say the word, and I'll send him off in a deserving manner. You needn't worry about Joya." He brushed some wild strands back off her face. "I'll not allow him to hurt you."

She shook her head and waved him off. "He couldn't hurt me if he tried."

Another look passed between husband and wife, and Alasdair leaned down to kiss Dyna's forehead and left.

Emmalin sat down on the other side of her on the bed. "Is he a bastard? Many of them are."

She couldn't help but chuckle over that accurate pronouncement. "Nay, he did naught wrong. 'Twas me. I did something I shouldn't have and I regret it."

"Do you wish to talk about it?"

Surprisingly she did, so she said in her usual blunt way, "I asked Derric to take my maidenhead." Her pledge to take her secret to the grave hadn't lasted long.

Emmalin didn't act the least bit shocked. "And did he oblige you?"

Confused by the possibility that he could have done such a thing so quickly, and well within view of the guards, she decided not to venture into that unknown territory. Best she didn't know, at this point. "He refused. Said it would never happen unless we were married or willing to marry."

"Good for Derric. 'Tis exactly what he should have said."

"Nay…" She'd hoped for a different response from the woman who'd laughed so bawdily earlier.

Emmalin reached for her hand and squeezed it. "I know you're curious, but you're of noble blood. If he wished to, our king could betroth you to a stranger, as he did with me. No one would dare try it since you're a Grant, but any man who steps in to relieve a laird's daughter of her virtue could be flogged, beaten, or killed. Is that what you wish to bring down on Derric? Because I think you just saw evidence from your cousin that Derric would have regretted it had he taken you up on your offer. I imagine you would have as well."

Dyna bolted up from the bed. "'Tis *my* maidenhead to give to whom I wish, no one else's."

"Dyna, one of the things I love about you is that you see things differently than most people. But you'll not find many men in this world who would agree with you about that. You're talking with a woman who was forced to marry an Englishman, and a cruel one at that. No one gave a fig about me except for the fact that I had my maidenhead. King Edward had no consideration for me at all. I was a pawn in a game of power. Don't be hurt by Derric's refusal. 'Tis the way of the world and he knows it."

"I suppose," she muttered. "But I *am* curious. My parents have always said that I can marry for love. And yet, I never thought it would happen. If we *do* marry… Claray wouldn't be able to handle it if we lived anywhere but Grant Castle." She paused, flustered, then admitted, "I don't know what to do. Derric makes me feel things I've not felt before, and I don't know how to handle myself with him. I feel like a young fool when I'm around him."

"Mayhap 'tis the excitement of new love you are feeling. I liked that feeling with Alasdair. Being close to him always made me feel butterflies were swarming my stomach. He was the only one who could make me giggle when times were the worst.

Whenever he was around, I believed in the good in the world. I don't know how better to explain it than that. If you feel that way with Derric, then think hard about sending him away. And as for his reaction to you, you do know that your cousins cornered him and threatened him with a wild boar, do you not?"

"What?" Dyna barked. He'd told her they'd warned him off, but they'd done it with a boar? Why couldn't they trust her to take care of her own business, to see to her own welfare?

"And your grandsire took him aside after that, though your cousins don't know what was said between them. Joya said her brother looked a wee bit green in the face after he returned."

Emmalin stood up, patted Dyna's shoulder, and said, "Don't take Derric's answer to heart. He was worried about keeping his bollocks, if I were to guess. And don't do something you may regret later."

No matter how much she wished to argue with Emmalin's points, she found she couldn't. Her friend was right. "My thanks for your honesty." Emmalin's descriptions of the butterflies perfectly matched the way Dyna felt whenever Derric was near. It had never happened with another man.

Was she falling in love with Derric Corbett?

Emmalin made her way to the door, then stopped and turned to look at her again, leaning on the door frame. "Are you going to send him away?"

"Nay," Dyna said. "He's brash and he doesn't know how to keep quiet, but I don't wish for him to leave. If he stays, 'twill be easier for me to discover the truth of my feelings. But I'll not ask him to take my maidenhead again. I can see 'twas too forward of me."

"Good. Don't rush it. Enjoy your time with him." Emmalin smiled and left.

How she wished her seer's abilities would come to the rescue now. Was Derric the one for her or not?

Unfortunately, she received no answer.

CHAPTER SEVEN

ERRIC WAS SO SHAKEN BY Dyna's question that he wasn't prepared to go back inside and face her cousins. He found his way to the stables, marching down to the end of the row until he saw a stable lad. "Have you any animals that are unsettled this eve? Any that are tough to put a saddle on or ornery in any way?" He liked a challenge, and working with horses calmed him. He needed that right now.

"Just Misty at the end. She prefers Lady Dyna, and whenever Dyna is upset, she gets upset," the lad said, pointing to the last stall. "I wouldn't go inside or she'll kick you, mayhap even try to bite you."

"Was Dyna here?"

"Nay, but Misty senses her mood. 'Tis uncanny the way it happens, but I've seen it many times. She needs a good brushing, but no one will go near her." Then he held out a brush, a hopeful expression on his face.

"I'll see what I can do, lad."

The lad smiled and ran off in the opposite direction, clearly less than confident in Derric's abilities. Derric searched for a barrel of treats and found an apple for the beast before heading down to the mare's stall. Once he got there, her ears moved back and she showed her teeth to him. It definitely didn't look like a smile. Opening the gate, she quickly came over and gave him a push, as if to tell him to leave her alone, but he started rubbing her withers, surprised that she allowed it so quickly. She took the proffered treat and chomped down on the apple, chewing slowly.

Derric continued, talking to her in a quiet voice, watching her teeth for that bite he'd been warned about, but she was too occupied by the apple to attempt it. Her movements were restless, even inside the stall. The stallion across the way gave a nicker, watching them.

"So that's why you're uncomfortable, aye?" Derric asked. He wants your attention and you aren't interested in him? Mayhap you sensed the same in your lady. She was upset with me, but not that upset. We had a lovely time together." He stopped rubbing her for a moment and she nudged him to continue.

Her movements slowly calmed, and she leaned into him, inviting him to pet her muzzle. He stroked it and brought the brush up to her neck. "Why, mayhap you're just exhausted. Has your mistress pushed you too hard? Or perhaps you *like* working hard. Are you ready to take her for another ride?" Misty nickered, as if to say aye, and he chuckled in response. "You aren't so mad now, are you? In fact, I'll find you another apple."

He left, and the horse tried to follow him, something that both delighted him and caught him by surprise. If a horse followed you, it usually meant they were fond of you, but he kept her inside the stall. He didn't wish to upset the big stallions nearby.

After grabbing a few more apples, he offered the treats to the beasts paying attention to him, each one nickering or nudging him with a thank you. Once he'd given the other treats out, he returned to Misty and gave her a soft hug. "You're much calmer than Dyna, or are you trying to tell me something about her? Her grandsire thinks she has a soft heart. What say you?" he whispered, speaking so low no one would hear him.

She whinnied and lifted her head, a gesture he chose to take as the horse's assent. "You answered that question so quickly, I wish you'd answer the rest of the ones that haunt me."

He was being utterly ridiculous, but he wished he had someone to talk with about Dyna. She had a way of making him want to be better. He'd worked out with his sword just to build up his body like the Grant warriors, and he'd be lying if he said the main reason wasn't to impress Dyna. She made him want to fight harder, run faster. She made him wish to be the kind of man Alexander Grant would want to marry his granddaughter.

Dyna made him dream of sharing a life with her. Of approaching her parents and asking for her hand in marriage. Of fighting side by side and then returning to their own cottage. Of having a bairn together.

And where would Senga fit into all of this? If not for the possibility that her lassie could be his daughter, she didn't fit in at all.

If his purpose had been to see if he and Dyna would suit, their time together on the hill had given him his answer. They were powerful together, even if he hadn't known how to answer the challenge she'd thrown at him. There was no denying that when he was with Dyna Grant, magic happened, and he believed she felt the same way.

He'd apologize to her later. He only hoped she could forgive him, because under no circumstances would he agree to take her maidenhead without marriage.

After he finished brushing Misty down, he returned to the great hall, sighing with relief when he found it empty. He hadn't wanted to see her cousins, true, but his greater fear was seeing the pain in Dyna's eyes. How could he explain himself to her?

Everything he'd said was true, but it didn't explain the entirety of his feelings. He wasn't worthy of a noblewoman. Her cousins didn't want him in the clan, or so it had felt in the middle of the woods with an angry wild boar aimed at him.

Dyna Grant tempted him more than any other woman. Her strength, her skills, her long legs. Her perfect arse. The way he could make her lose all sense. Making a lass like Dyna fall apart in his arms, moan with need, beg him for more…it was more than a man could ever wish for, was it not?

But he could have a daughter somewhere with a camp woman. And part of him thought he shouldn't commit himself to Dyna until he knew the truth of that.

Joya and Els came in from the kitchens just then, so he bolted up out of his chair. Joya gave him a searching look and said, "Everything all right, Derric? You disappeared."

The last thing he wanted to do was open his heart to Els, who'd made it clear that he didn't think much of him, so he just shrugged.

To his surprise, Els gave Joya a kiss on her cheek and said, "I'm going to run out to the stables. I'll be back in a few minutes." He nodded to Derric before he left. The gesture was a surprisingly kind one, and there didn't look to be any spite or judgment in his eyes.

Turning to Joya, Derric said, "Sit with me awhile?"

Joya sat down and tipped her head at him. "Something's bothering you, I can tell."

He sighed. "Aye, many things. First, a general question for you. How would you describe a person who's soft-hearted?" He hadn't forgotten the fact that he had a quest to complete before Alex would consent to their marriage.

She didn't question why he was asking, which he was grateful for—she thought it through instead. "Emmalin is soft-hearted. She's warm and loving and wonderful with the bairns. She's verra good at sympathizing with anyone who has a problem. She gives warm hugs and good advice."

While she'd wished to help Coira, most of those characteristics didn't fit Dyna. She didn't play with the bairns much, though she wasn't bad with them either. She didn't spend much time talking to people she didn't know well. In fact, she spent much of her time alone or with her cousins. That answer didn't help his quest at all, so he thought of something else.

"May I tell you something in confidence?" he whispered, still afraid he'd be overheard.

"Aye, I'll not tell anyone."

"King Robert told me one of the camp lasses I knew was searching for me. Apparently she now has a daughter. Robert said she was heading north. I intend to find her."

Joya's brow arched at that comment, not that he blamed her. He wasn't proud of the situation, but he wished to be honest. It was the only way she could help him.

"Are you saying 'tis possible the babe is yours?"

"Possible? Aye. 'Tis not likely, but the only way I'll know for certain is to ask Senga. See the child for myself."

"And if she says you're the sire?" She kept her hands folded in her lap, something he knew Joya did to keep from announcing her emotions. She'd told him once that it was something she'd learned as a spy.

"I should probably marry her." He glanced at her to see her reaction, but she held steady. "I'm sure 'tis what Papa would say if he were here."

"I'm not sure what to say. You haven't really asked me anything, and you haven't told me if the prospect of fatherhood pleases you nor how you feel about this lass. You also haven't told me about the most important thing happening to you at present."

He scratched his head, standing up to pace in front of the hearth. "I've always wanted bairns, but…" He took a swig of ale and set the goblet down, nearly knocking it over. "Where would we settle down? We don't have a clan and Senga mustn't have one either."

"Derric, you would always be welcome here. Alasdair and Emmalin are trying hard to build their own clan on MacLintock land. I love it here. 'Tis my home. You'd be asked to fight as a guard or some other contribution, but they'd be happy for you to stay." She smiled at him, her emotions finally bleeding through into her expression. "I'd love to have you in my life again."

"You would? And you think they'd agree?" Another thought occurred to him, and he stopped his pacing in front of her. "I must return to something else. What were you speaking of earlier when you mentioned the most important thing happening to me now?"

"You just asked me three questions," she said with a small smile. "Of course I would like you in my life. You are my only remaining family and I love you. And you *would* be welcome here. And as for your last question, I'm going to pry as any good sister should. Do you not have strong feelings for Dyna? I notice you cannot take your gaze from her, wherever we are."

"I do," he said, taking up his pacing again. "Verra much, but I don't know if I can ask anything of her until I find out the truth about Senga's daughter. 'Struth, I was hoping Dyna might be willing to go north with me after seeing Alex to Cameron land. We need another archer in King Robert's camp right now, and I think we'd both like to spend time with each other without her clan around. But how do I ask her to come with me if I'm looking for another woman at the same time?"

"And if you discover that Senga's daughter is your bairn? How will Dyna feel if you end up offering for someone else?"

He closed his eyes because that was exactly his fear. But he'd come here anyway—because he'd wished to see Joya too, but also because he'd needed to see Dyna. In his heart, he hoped the bairn wasn't his, that he might have a life with Dyna, but...

"Sister, I'm not of noble blood. She is. I doubt her sire or her grandsire would welcome me as a suitor. Your husband and his cousin have not been warm to me, and Alex himself pulled me aside and warned me to guard her soft heart. Said he would send me away if I did not. I doubt any of them would be pleased to see the two of us together."

"Derric, your blood is the same as mine. No one questioned me or made me feel unwelcome, and look what my past was like. They're an open-minded clan and I think you'd suit Dyna verra well. You're more alike than you may realize. Please don't dismiss the possibility of a relationship with her. She's interested in you. That is clear to see."

"Did Alex Grant welcome you to the clan?"

"Aye, he's verra kind to me." She gave him a pointed look. "You need to pay more attention to all that takes place here. Have you had a serious interest in any other lass? Have you felt stronger feelings for anyone besides Dyna? Even Senga?"

"Nay." He knew that one word spoke more about what he should do than any other. Dyna was the one for him. If he just hadn't had this complication arise, the threat from her cousins, even the conversation with her grandsire nearly made him question everything.

"You need no other answer, brother. 'Tis the truth of it there."

He stopped his pacing and said, "You are right, and I know it." Earning the respect of Alex Grant would be his first quest, and he had to hope that if he did, the cousins would follow. He ran his hand down his face then looked directly into his sister's eyes. He had one more important issue that continued to niggle at him. The only way to settle it was to know the truth. "I have another question for you. Do you hate me for leaving you behind?" He started pacing again because he feared seeing the truth in her eyes.

"Nay. I was much too young to go with you, Derric. And I needed to deal with losing our parents. Besides, Auntie wouldn't have welcomed you. I heard her tell someone else she was glad you moved on."

He shrugged. "I knew she didn't want me there. Still, I should have stayed for your sake." He sat on the arm of a chair, his shoulders drooping. There, he'd finally said it. "It was wrong of me to leave you, whatever the circumstances."

To his surprise, Joya went to him and wrapped her arms around him, setting her head on his shoulder. "Derric, nay. I wish Mama and Papa had lived, but since they did not, what happened was for the best. You would not have been happy living with us. That much I know. You were too mature, too set in your ways."

"Joya, I'm deeply sorry if I hurt you. I really did miss you."

She waved her hand at him as she moved back to her chair. "'Tis in the past. I don't wish to look backward. I want to see you happily married and with someone who doesn't live far away. To my mind, Dyna would be perfect for you."

Derric stood, set his hands on his hips, and said, "I don't wish to hurt Dyna. Believe me. I know 'tis a risk to travel with her, not knowing what I'll learn about the bairn. But if I leave on a long journey and don't return until spring, I fear I'll find her wed to some noble fop unworthy of her. I'd want to put a fist in his foppy face."

Joya smirked and waggled her brow at her brother. "'Tis the most telling statement you've made yet. Who would be worthy of Dyna? I think you just answered your own question. There's only one person she belongs with, is there not?"

He pursed his lips with a renewed vigor. "Aye.

Me."

Dyna sat next to her grandsire at the trestle table the next morn, long before Joya typically woke up. Emmalin was still abovestairs with the bairns. Alasdair and Els were in the lists and servants meandered about, cleaning the hall and preparing it for the day ahead. Derric entered from outside, and Alex's sharp eyes instantly flew to him. "Join us, Corbett. I'll have the serving lass bring porridge and bread for us."

Dyna wondered what her grandsire was about, but she didn't comment. Rather, she conveyed her grandsire's wishes to a nearby serving lass. Derric sat down and nodded to her. "Good morn to you, lass."

It was the first she'd seen him since their discussion on the hill. Part of her had worried he might be gone, that her offer—and his refusal—would drive him away. Mayhap he still intended to leave.

"Corbett, I am headed to Cameron land later today," Grandsire said. "I promised my sister a visit, and I intend to keep my word. Will you join us? Dyna will travel to Grant land after that, and I'd like to ask you to escort her. There will be a number of guards along, of course. But I'd like someone she trusts to go with her." Three bowls of porridge were set on the table, along with a small bowl of honey to enhance the flavor and some fresh bread. "Where were you planning to go after your visit with Joya?"

"North. I'm going to join King Robert's forces. He's expecting me back within a sennight."

"Will you travel with us?" the old man asked, fussing with his food instead of looking at him.

Dyna hadn't expected that proposal at all. Would Derric accept? He'd said that he wished for her to travel north with him, yet they'd both parted unhappy with each other the previous night. Truthfully, Dyna wanted him to come along. If he didn't, she feared she might never see him again.

He surprised her by being direct. "Dyna, what say you?"

"You are welcome to join us," she said. "I may spend a night on Cameron land before moving on. You need not follow me to Grant land."

Grandsire gave her that look that told her he wouldn't accept any other option. "I'm asking him to follow you to Grant land. There have been enough attacks on members of my family lately that I would prefer to know you are safe. If he's willing, I ask you to accept it quietly, Dyna."

Dyna's jaw tensed. Her grandfather rarely spoke to her that way. Most of the time he asked her about her preferences rather than ordering her about. She opened her mouth to argue, but her grandfather gave her another of his looks.

"Corbett?" Grandsire prompted.

"Of course. I'd be honored and pleased to travel with you."

"Good, 'tis settled. Now, do you wish to explain what has happened between you two to cause this rift?"

Dyna nearly fell off her bench. Hellfire, why did the wily old man have to be so astute all the time? She was supposed to be the one with seer abilities, but those abilities sure had been failing her when it came to Derric Corbett. Perhaps she'd lost them.

Grandsire gave her a kindly look. "It doesn't take a seer to figure out that you two are having an issue, Dyna."

Dammit, but he could even read her mind. *Her* mind!

Corralling her senses to come up with a good answer, she hid her hands in her lap. "I don't know of what you speak, Grandsire. There's no trouble between us. Do you not agree, Derric?"

Derric coughed, but he didn't disagree. "Aye. Dyna's a fine friend."

The sound of the wee ones echoed through the hall as John and Coira came down the staircase, Emmalin and Ailith behind them.

Grandfather stood up and said, "I'm taking my porridge to the hearth. I'll eat with the bairns, enjoy their company before we leave." He gathered his things, then looked from one to the other. "Mend whatever has gone wrong between you. You'll get along and work together when we're on the road. You won't want my prying *or* my interference."

As Grandsire moved toward the hearth, his meal in hand, John shouted out, "*Seanair.* You have porridge? Shall I find some for Coira, too?"

"Aye, laddie. There's enough in this bowl for both you and Coira. And here's some bread for each of you, too. The lasses will bring your goat's milk."

"*Seanair*, I be big and strong like Papa."

"You will if you drink your milk and eat your porridge," Grandsire said with a smile.

John picked up his sword and swung it three times in front of the hearth while he waited for his milk. "See, Coira. I warrey already."

Dyna couldn't help but smirk over John's attempt to say "warrior." She glanced over at Derric to see if he'd noticed. His gaze was locked on the trio by the hearth, as were the others in the hall. John and *Seanair* were truly a favorite. Grandsire would be missed when he left.

John let out his best attempt at the Grant war whoop followed by a wee growl. That sent her grandsire into a deep chuckle.

Then she recalled what the man had said to the two of them. A rift. He'd known something had gone awry. How she prayed he had no true inkling of what she'd done. Dyna swallowed and stared at Derric, wondering how he would react to Grandsire's bold statement.

Handsome bastard. Being this close to Derric sent her heart aflutter. Traitorous heart. She hadn't yet adjusted to his closeness, his scent inspiring her to remember exactly how it felt to have his lips and hands roaming all over her body.

"You could have denied him if my presence upsets you," Derric said softly.

"Deny Grandsire?" she snorted. "That does not happen." She stared at her hands in her lap under the table. "Derric, forgive me for being so forward.

I probably shouldn't have said what I did."

"You did surprise me, but 'struth is I was humbled and flattered by your request. I think you know that there's nothing I'd like better than to do as you asked, but…"

He had an expression on his face she'd never seen before. His usual arrogance was gone, replaced by a vulnerability that she found oddly appealing. "But?"

"But my sire taught me about honor and responsibility. While I haven't seen him in many years, he did impress many things on me, thick as my head might be. At times, I wish I could forget his lessons, but they rear up when I least expect it. I believe in heaven, and my goal is to get there someday so I can see my parents again. So I can make them proud. Your cousins and your grandsire reminded me of my parents and their teachings. Which is why I cannot do as you asked. I'd also like to earn the respect of your clan someday. If I did *that*, I never would."

"So you'll forgive my crudeness?" She couldn't hide her smirk.

He gave her a crooked smile and said, "Aye, even if you've made it even harder not to touch you. I would like to get along with you, Dyna."

"I'd like that, too. I admit I watched you in the lists with Alasdair this morn. Your sword skills are improving, and I would be pleased to have you along to help me protect Grandsire."

Because she wanted to protect Grandsire as much as he wanted to protect her.

"But your grandsire said you'd be taking guards."

"Aye, a group of them will be accompanying us, but they do not have the sword skills you have. I need someone who can hold any attackers off while I get into the trees to get a better angle for my arrows."

"Understood. I'll be ready and by the gates." Derric nodded and left, taking a hunk of bread with him.

Dyna breathed a sigh of relief. She wasn't ready to lose him. Not yet.

An odd thought echoed in her mind, the way they sometimes did.

Not ever.

CHAPTER EIGHT

D ERRIC WAS PLEASED THEY GAVE him a
fine stallion to ride, not up to the same stan-
dards as Midnight, but a fine steed nonetheless.
Before they left, he'd spent time stroking the beast
and giving him the chance to get to know his rider.

He'd said goodbye to his sister, pleased he no
longer had to worry about her. She hadn't let him
get away without a little taunt. "I hope you come
back firmly attached to a tall, willowy blonde."

He'd taunted back. "I hope I come back to find
you with a big round belly. I'd love a niece or a
nephew." He'd kissed her cheek, then said, "Mayhap both."

She'd slapped his arm playfully and said, "Go and
Godspeed. Take care of my cousin."

He'd listened to the guards conversing with
Alasdair and Alex, taking in all the strategizing
that probably took place before every journey the
Grants ever took. Planned stops, expected compli-
cations, alternate routes—they'd discussed every
possible complication. English garrisons, reivers,

wild boars, who knew what was in the Highlands these days? They expected to arrive on Cameron land around nightfall, so they would only need to stop once to freshen the horses and take care of their own needs.

Dyna rode her beautiful horse, Misty, but Derric had to admit, he only had eyes for the rider. But they were traveling with Alex, which was a painful reminder that he had yet to complete the quest he'd been assigned, because he hadn't uncovered one soft thing about the lass besides her skin, and he very much doubted that was what Alex Grant had in mind.

The trip was uneventful until they were about an hour from the safety of Cameron land and the horses began to fuss. Alex ordered the group to stop so they could listen for any evidence of what was upsetting the animals.

The sound of hoofbeats carried to them, the number large enough for Alex to announce, "'Tis a full garrison of soldiers, probably English. Dismount and get down."

He no sooner finished his sentence than the sound of thunder of the approaching horses grew louder, as if the garrison was headed directly for them. They reined in their horses and raced into a copse of trees for cover.

Derric stayed behind Dyna, who tried to climb into a tree but was stopped by her bellowing grandfather. "Dyna, we cannot take on a cavalry that large. On the ground!"

She raced to a hiding spot, and Derric was about

to do the same when Alex stopped him mid-step. "Corbett, you'll protect my granddaughter."

Derric switched his direction and followed Dyna into a well-hidden spot behind a clump of bushes. She went flat on her belly and he lowered himself next to her.

"What the hell? You need not protect me."

"I don't argue with your grandsire. Do you?" he growled through clenched teeth. "Especially when we're about to be set upon by a mass of Englishmen."

She snarled and mumbled incomprehensible words until he reached over and placed his hand over her mouth. "Quiet. You can curse me later."

Her glance was one of fury, that fiery look of hers that he loved, but neither of them said anything because the horses' hooves were now booming all around them. Their copse had to be in the middle of the cavalry's path.

Her fury changed to a brief look of fear that unmanned him. So he did the only thing he could think to do. He cupped her face and moved closer, his lips meeting hers with an urgency and a need that he couldn't hide.

Bloody hell, but the lass did things to him he couldn't comprehend. He thought she'd push him away, but instead she nipped his lower lip, something that drove him mad. He grabbed her shoulders and maneuvered her underneath him, ravaging her lips until she arched against him, then she wrapped her arms around his neck and tugged him closer.

It was a duel of tongues he didn't care if he ever won, her assault on his lips as powerful as his own on hers. Hellfire, what would the lass be like in bed?

Explosive. If their kissing was any indication of what their lovemaking would be, it would be beyond anything he'd ever experienced. He stopped for a moment to catch his breath. "Are you trying to kill me, lass?"

"'Tis a far sight better than listening to the English cavalry come closer. I'd rather die wrapped in your arms than alone."

He set his finger to her lips, doing his best to listen between the panting breaths coming from both of them.

The sounds had decreased, indicating the English had passed their location and were no longer a threat. Derric sat up from the ground cover that had concealed them, keeping his hand on her shoulder to keep her down until he checked the area.

As if that would work.

She bolted up next to him, her hair in disarray around her face, pulled out of her plait from their tumble. The others stood up, so Derric grabbed Dyna's hand and helped her to her feet.

"Grandsire, you are hale?" she asked in a low tone.

"Aye, I'm fine." She rushed over to help him, but he waved her off. "I can get myself up."

She stepped back, and the other guards went to retrieve their horses.

"Did you see them, Grandsire?"

"Nay, and I'm sure you two didn't see a thing." He cast them a knowing look and went after Midnight.

Dyna blushed and froze. Derric waited until Alex had retrieved his mount before he went after their horses, bringing Dyna's beast along with his own. When he reached her side, he leaned down to whisper in her ear. "Hellfire, does the man miss naught?"

Dyna just arched a brow at him with a snort.

"I have to learn to be more careful," he said, saying it for others to hear, hoping he'd convince himself of the importance of that creed. He was too lax from spending most of his life around camp men and warriors.

One of the guards said, "They were definitely English. Where do you think they're headed?"

"No idea." Alex mounted his horse and made his way out to the trampled meadow. "At least a hundred." He glanced over at Derric and said, "Mayhap they're headed toward wherever they think King Robert is."

Derric lifted Dyna up onto her horse, surprised she didn't balk, but she did pinch his finger. He wished to laugh because he knew the only reason she'd accepted his assistance was because of her grandfather.

He'd turned toward his own horse when one of the guards behind him said, "Corbett, your lip is bleeding. You run into a bush or something?"

He yanked his tunic up and wiped his lip, surprised to see the amount of blood there. He glanced back at Dyna, who smirked at him, but her amusement quickly fled. He followed her gaze and saw she had focused on his abdomen. He intentionally lifted his tunic a bit higher, wiping the sweat from his brow.

Her face flushed with heat, which was gratifying but not exactly the response he'd hoped for.

She wriggled in her seat.

He wanted to roar and pound his chest in victory.

Instead, he dropped his shirt and strode back to her. The others were moving about, so he'd not be heard. He rested his hand on her calf and squeezed. "Be careful, lass."

"What?" That glare had returned, but he couldn't stop himself.

"You're squirming in your saddle, Diamond."

He sauntered back to his horse.

But not before a stone hit the back of his head, followed by a chuckle of her laughter.

The rest of the journey passed quickly, and before they knew it, the rocky landscape told them they were nearly on Cameron land. Dyna breathed a sigh of relief, knowing that Grandsire would be safely ensconced with his youngest sister. Aunt Jennie would help him with his ailments, something he needed once or twice a year of late. She always sent home plenty of ointments and poultices with him, both for him and for others who might suffer injuries or illnesses in the clan.

To their surprise, a group of horses came forward to meet them, Uncle Aedan in the lead, his brother Ruari next to him.

He made his way to Grandsire's horse and stopped. "Greetings to you, Alex. Your sister is anxious to see you."

"And I'm anxious to see her. I'm glad you received our message. We made a quick decision, but I hope you have room for us for a night or two. Most of the Grant warriors will continue on to Grant land with my granddaughter, but I'll stay on with a few men if you'll have us."

"Of course. My wife's favorite brother is always welcome. Had you any problems with your journey?"

"One large English garrison moved past us, but we saw no others. Why? You don't often ride out to greet us, Cameron." She could see the suspicious look on his wizened face, and Uncle Aedan must have seen it, too, because he chuckled.

"Quite true. We've received word there are two English garrisons heading north, though they have orders to stay far away from Lochluin Abbey. I suspect they're the ones you saw, but there's to be another behind them. There are also two groups of Scottish Lowlanders heading that direction to support Bruce's enemies—Macdougall and Ross. Wanted to advise the rest of your group in case you had other plans."

Dyna said, "We can stay for one night and be on our way at first light."

Aedan's brow furrowed. "'Twill put you right in the middle. The other English group will be traveling past Cameron land on the morrow, to pass here by midday."

"You have to leave now," Grandsire said, to her complete surprise.

"But Grandsire, can we not sleep first?"

"Nay. 'Tis out of the question. Corbett, I'm asking you to see my granddaughter straight to Grant land. Turning back to Dyna, he said, "The moon is full, you can get through the treacherous ravine now. You'll want to be on the other side of it before those men come through. You know how to pass it safely, but they'll be tied up there all day. Besides, I can feel a storm coming, and if you get on the far side of the ravine, there are several deep caves, one that can hold horses. Get there before you sleep."

Alex spoke to their guards, splitting them up. A few would stay with him on Cameron land, and the rest would continue on to Grant Castle.

Dyna couldn't believe Grandsire was sending them along so quickly. She was already exhausted from the journey and wished to sleep, but she saw the wisdom in it too, and didn't wish to get caught by the English. She was ready to be home, to see her parents and siblings.

Aedan said, "Dyna, we suspected you might decide to carry on with your journey, so Jennie sent a skin of ale and a sack of dried meat and cheese for you. She also included a few things for the Grant healers.

One of Aedan's guards dismounted and took care

of the transfer of goods from one horse to others. Dyna tucked the healer's goods into her saddlebag.

"Oh, and two new fox furs for your trip," Aedan added. "'Twill get cold and we've had many made."

She glanced at her grandsire, her heart breaking because they would be parted—for who knew how long—but she had to share him with his many siblings and grandbairns. "Grandsire, be truthful with Aunt Jennie about your needs. Stay for as long as you like. I'll return for you whenever you send a message."

"I will, Dyna. Godspeed and listen to Corbett. He's wiser than you give him credit for."

Her grandfather turned his horse and rode toward Cameron land alongside Aedan.

Dyna's group set out, too, and she couldn't help but turn around and wave several times until they were out of sight.

She had an uncanny feeling that this could be the last time she saw her grandfather.

CHAPTER NINE

THEY FOLLOWED ALEX'S ADVICE AND got to the ravine quickly, which was for the best, because he'd been right about the weather. A cold wind had come out of nowhere, scattering leaves across the landscape, and judging from the fast clouds and the ominous gray sky, the storm would be upon them within the hour. Once they were safely on the other side, they could spend the night in a cave and leave in the morning after the storm passed. If all went well, they could arrive on Grant land well before dusk—ahead of the English, who would probably get caught before the ravine, which would become treacherous to cross in the storm.

The rain began pelting them halfway across. Derric sent Dyna across ahead of him, knowing she knew the terrain better than any of them, and the guards trailed behind them.

"Don't slow," he said. "'Twill only get worse. Don't worry about us, get yourself across."

By the time they got to the other side, they were

drenched to the bone. Dyna continued on ahead, for she knew exactly where to locate the cave Alex had mentioned.

The trek took forever, but Dyna finally motioned them down a small path that emptied into a clearing near a burn. The cave was to the right of the burn, tucked under a ledge of rock, and she dismounted in front of it and took in her saddlebag.

Derric found a dry area beneath an outcropping for the beasts. He saw to both his horse and Misty, giving them both sacks of oats, and then turned to address the guards. "Take care of your animals."

He hurried into the cave, grabbing some of their belongings from the pack horse in the hopes they would dry by the fire. His clothes were drenched clear through, and a whoosh of air escaped his lips once he stepped inside the shelter, away from nature's fury.

But he forgot his own discomfort the moment his gaze found Dyna, huddled against the cave wall. "Derric, help me." She was shivering so hard her teeth chattered.

He dropped his belongings in a dry spot and hurried over to her. "Lass, you have the look of a fever." Her eyes had a dull, glazed look, one he'd seen in others taken by the fever. Her skin had a sheen of what he guessed to be sweat, not rain, and her lips were unnaturally pale.

"I'm cold." Her shoulders shook uncontrollably, but when he reached out to touch her, she felt hot. He jerked his hands back. "And my head is paining me terribly. Can you not start a fire?"

"Bloody hell, you're sick."

"Help me. Please. I can't move. I need to get something warm."

"Lass, I'll help you undress before the others come inside. You have to get out of those wet clothes." She stood there, helpless, her eyes glassy with the fever. "Take your mantle off."

Three of the guards entered. One of them, Ham, said, "'Tis nasty out there," shaking his head, his wet hair throwing off drops of water.

His eyes widened when he saw Dyna. "She doesn't look good." He rubbed his chin. "I'll fill the skins and look for dry wood."

Derric said, "Aye, we need to start a fire. A big one. We have to dry off." He pointed to a spot near the entrance, where the fire would be close enough to the opening for them to keep most of the smoke out of the cave but far enough not to fall prey to the elements. "Build the fire there. I'm taking her around this bend to get her out of these wet clothes. Stay the hell away."

Ham smirked. "I'll help." His gaze carried the innocent look of a babe in a swaddling cloth.

"The hell you will." Derric gave him a menacing look, but it was Dyna's threat that sent him scurrying away—

"Come near me, any of you, and I'll fire an arrow into your bollocks the moment I'm better."

Ham spun on his heel, shoving at the backs of the guards in front of him, the other men having already turned to see about the fire. The others must have teased him because their laughter carried across the storm.

"Get as much dry kindling as you can find. There was a thick group of pines just behind the outcropping. There could be some dry wood there."

The guards left, speaking to the men who were still outside, and Derric ushered Dyna around the bend. "Here, give me your mantle. Do you have a dry set of leggings?"

"Aye, in my sack. And a tunic."

Derric searched the sacks Dyna had brought in. To his surprise, everything was dry inside the bags given to them by the Camerons. It was far better than any sack he'd ever used. He pulled the two furs out, tossing one to Dyna. "Cover yourself with this while you undress."

A long ledge sat at the side, so Derric unpacked the sacks, setting everything out. The food from the Camerons came first, then some containers of poultices and salves, another fur, and finally the tunic and leggings from Dyna's bag.

When he finished and closed the bags, he turned around to Dyna and froze. She stood there with nothing on, shivering in the cold, trying to warm herself with the fur she'd wrapped around her female parts, her long willowy legs shaking. Her bound breasts drew his eye.

"Derric, you have to help me unbind this. It's so wet it's rubbing my skin raw."

Bloody hell, he was about to put himself into a torture chamber.

"I'll help you. Put the dry leggings on first."

"I don't know if I can." Her weak, thready voice

terrified. "I think I'll fall over." He'd rather she curse at him in three different ways.

"I'll stand in front of you, give you my back, and you can lean against me."

"I'll try."

He did as he promised, doing his best not to think of her long legs, or the curly junction of her thighs, or the soft globes of her backside.

She set her shoulder against him and nearly fell. He stuck his arm out straight. "Hold onto my arm."

"I have one leg in." Her hand wrapped around him, and he had to close his eyes to control his reaction.

She started to fall again, so he cursed and turned around, grabbing her armpits from behind to steady her. He got a glimpse of the sweet curves of her backside just before he closed his eyes again. It took every speck of will he possessed not to groan, but somehow he managed it. He'd be up for sainthood for sure after this.

"Get the leggings on," he said, his voice hoarse.

Once her leggings were on, she unhooked the binding around her breasts, keeping her back to him, and handed the end of the cloth to him so he could assist her in unwinding the cursed band.

"Just warning you they aren't the large breasts most men like."

He snapped, "I'm not most men."

She reached for the dry tunic on the stone floor and put it on, keeping her back to him. When she was finally covered, he let out a long breath he'd been holding through the entire ordeal.

He'd survived.

The men returned and worked on the fire, two of them bringing skins back to Derric and Dyna, one of fresh water from the burn and one of ale.

She reached for the water, but Derric took it first. "We'll be heating that before anyone drinks it. Robert says water straight from a burn is less likely to make you heave if you heat it first. Have a sip or two of Cameron ale. 'Tis less likely to upset your belly."

Once the fire was started, Ham announced, "I'm exhausted. I'll have a piece of cheese, and I'm bedding down for the night."

The others agreed, and they got situated on the floor of the cave. Dyna had a couple of bites of cheese then folded up one of the furs and rested her head on it. She was asleep within minutes. Derric took the other fur and covered her up.

He fell asleep not long after.

A crack of thunder, so close the ground shook, awakened him in the night. He glanced over at Dyna and could see her trembling even in the dark. Soft moans came from her lips.

Moving over to her side, he felt her skin, the fever raging through her. "I'm so cold," she mumbled in her sleep.

Derric couldn't stand to watch her suffer. He'd removed his tunic and set it to dry by the fire, but he had his extra dry plaid as a blanket. Hoping he wouldn't awaken her, he settled himself behind her and tucked her backside up against him, giving her his heat, and wrapped his arms around her. He didn't know what else to do to help her, but at least he could try to keep her warm. The body was strange in the way it could shiver from cold even as it felt hot to the touch. He would do what he could to help her.

Losing her was not an option.

CHAPTER TEN

W HEN DYNA AWAKENED, SHE WAS in a
soft bed, far away from the dark cave she'd
fallen asleep in. She forced herself to a sitting position and moaned, holding her head in an attempt
to soothe the powerful ache. It felt like one of the
fae was beating inside her head with a tiny mallet.

Her sister, Claray, sat across from her. "Dyna? You
are hale?" Her voice was both intent and worried,
the pitch higher than usual.

"Claray? Where am I? What's wrong?"

"You were sick. I was afraid you were dying.
Please promise me you'll never die. I cannot lose
you." She could see the tears welling up in her
sister's eyes.

"I'm on Grant land? How did I get here?"

Her sister moved to sit on the bed, reaching for
her hand. The expression on her face told Dyna
exactly how sick she must have been. She'd not
seen that shade of fear on Claray's face during the
day, only at night, after she'd awoken from one of
her nightmares. "You're in your chamber. Der-

ric brought you here last eve with a raging fever. Aunt Gracie and Mama bathed you and gave you a potion. How do you feel?"

"Awful." She reached up to massage her pounding temple. "There was an awful storm, but we made it through the ravine and into the cave before…" Memories began to return to her—memories of *him*. She recalled Derric helping her to undress, giving her the furs, supporting her.

She had an odd sense of sleeping next to his heat, his arms tightly wrapped around her. Was her mind playing tricks on her? "Derric? Is he still here?"

"Aye, he said he would stay two eves before he left. He wanted to make sure you were hale. Is he something to you, Dyna?" Claray looked down at her hands, worrying them. "Are you leaving me? You always said you'd never marry, but he seems…"

A knock interrupted her, saving Dyna from having to answer the question. "Enter."

Her mother came in and sat down on the opposite side of the bed. How do you feel?" Sela Grant was still a statuesque beauty.

"Terrible. I guess I had the fever. I remember shivering, but I don't remember how I got from the cave to here."

Her mother patted her arm. "Derric protected you and carried you inside. You rode in front of him. He said you slept the entire way, shivering on and off."

"I'll have to thank him," she mumbled before she dropped back onto the bed. "My head is killing me." She rolled onto her side and closed her eyes.

"Your father and I thanked him profusely. We could tell he'd taken good care of you. Had you been alone, you would have fallen off your horse and never been found. Remember this when you think on running off on your own again." Her mother got up and covered her. "I'll get something for your head from Aunt Gracie. She said Aunt Jennie sent some new potions and poultices. Your father wishes to speak with you, so he'll bring it up. Rest your eyes until then. I'll send a warm bowl of porridge for you, too." Then she stopped for a moment. "You can thank Derric yourself. You *should* thank him when you're feeling hale. He's a fine young man."

Dyna nodded and closed her eyes, falling into oblivion again.

The next time she opened her eyes, her sire stood next to her bed. He set a small table next to her and arranged the porridge and the potion on it. "Aunt Gracie sent this for you."

"My thanks, Papa," she mumbled. How she'd missed him. Even though he had a well-deserved reputation as a fierce warrior, he had a soft heart, a propensity to see the good in everyone.

He helped her sit up, propping pillows behind her before handing her the potion and the bowl of porridge. "You need to eat something after you take the potion. Derric said you were in bad condition."

She swallowed two bites, the heat easing some of the pain in her throat.

Her father waited for her to swallow before he

continued his inquisition.

"Grandsire. Derric told me what he knows, but I'd prefer to hear it from you." He sat back, giving her a chance to gather her thoughts. He was never one to be pushy or overly insistent. He was almost as patient as his father, though not quite. Grandsire had the patience of a saintly priest, and how he did it, no one knew.

"Two sheriffs arrived at MacLintock Castle to warn Grandsire that Edward's son was sending out garrisons after him. He decided to go to Cameron land. Although he didn't explain his reasoning, I suspect he thought it less likely they'd think to look for him there. I know he didn't wish to bring any more battles to MacLintock Castle. You know Grandsire. He worries, especially over the wee ones."

"Did you know the sheriffs? Scottish or English?"

"Busby and DeFry. Both are Scottish, and they claim allegiance to King Robert. I trust DeFry and so does Alasdair. Busby we don't know as well. We met him in Berwick."

Her sire rubbed his jaw in thought. "Derric said King Robert is headed north and he plans to join up with him as soon as you're hale. What are your plans once you've healed?"

"Papa, I'd like to go with Derric, see what is happening in the north." She watched her father, the man she so adored for all he'd done for her family—rescuing her mother and Claray, finding a home for the orphans Thorn and Nari, who now lived with her uncle Loki.

"Why?" Leave it to her father to keep his words short. And really, it was just as well with her pounding head.

"I can't explain it, but I have a feeling something important is about to happen in the Highlands. And I know it will not happen here. I dreamed that I was chasing someone on horseback. Derric is heading north. Perhaps I need to travel with him to see what is happening with King Robert. According to Uncle Aedan, there were two garrisons of Englishmen and two groups of Lowlanders traveling north."

"Did you know who you were chasing?" Her parents trusted her seer abilities. They'd learned from experience that her hunches were always right.

"I know what you're asking. Was it Grandsire? Perhaps. And yet, I felt two conflicting premonitions on Cameron land. One was that Cameron land was the safest place he could go, especially with Lochluin Abbey so close. I believed it was a good decision." She stopped to massage her head, hoping more premonitions would come, though she knew it was unlikely with such an ache in her head.

"And the other?"

"When I waved to Grandsire, I had the odd feeling that it would be the last I saw of him for a long time. That made me ill. I tried to open myself to more premonitions, but then the fever took over. I couldn't stop it. I was so cold in the rain."

She waited for his counsel because he always

gave such good advice. He and Uncle Jamie had a rare ability to see down to the core of an issue. She'd said as much to her sire, but he'd told her it was a talent born of experience.

"No reason to think on it anymore. I've told you that you need to allow them to come to you in their own good time. Molly always told us that you cannot rush such things. They come to you or they do not." He peered at her, then asked, "Do you have an interest in this Derric? I've not minded you traveling with your cousins, but this man is not related to you."

"Papa, there were Grant guards with us, just as there will be if we go north together. And nay, I have no interest in him." The lie had spilled out of her so easily, without any premeditation, and she understood why—her father would never let her travel with Derric if he knew the truth. "Grandsire made him promise to bring me to Grant land. He was with us for much of the journey."

"So he must trust him, which is a good sign. I'm aware of the presence of the guards, but I was young, too. He gave you his heat when you were shivering, did he not?"

"Aye, but I barely recall it. I was too sickly. He acted honorably."

"Good to hear. But I'd like to have a chat with young Derric," her father said, rising from his chair. "You sleep. You're going nowhere in your present condition."

She knew what that meant—yet another of her relatives was about to threaten Derric, and her father was the most intimidating of all. He'd probably run like the wind.

She rested her head down on the pillow and murmured, "Papa?"

"Aye?"

"He's already been threatened by Alasdair and Els, plus Grandsire had a long talk with him. Please don't frighten him away."

His father smiled. "Then he does mean something to you."

She sighed, unable to deny what her heart told her. "Aye, I do like him. I must thank him for bringing me safely home."

Would that convince her father to stand down? She could only hope.

Derric was in the lists, practicing with Alick. Although he'd been impressed with the men on MacLintock land, Grant land was another world. The warriors here had sword skills the likes of which he'd never seen. And the land itself…

He enjoyed the view of the snow-topped mountains and had even ridden out to the loch earlier, the water rippling in the wind in a way that calmed his soul.

A strange thought had passed through his head on the heels of that one.

He could spend his life in a place like this.

"Pay attention," Alick said. "Is your mind wandering, or are you just thinking of Dyna?" He smirked as he said it, but at least he hadn't threatened him with a wild boar. Yet.

The tallest man he'd ever seen stalked toward them, his gaze directed at Derric. He knew without asking that it had to be Dyna's sire. He'd heard about Connor Grant's sword skills and his abilities as a leader of Clan Grant. He also bore an uncanny resemblance to his father, Alex, and to Dyna. If he wondered why Dyna was so tall for a lass, the answer stood in front of him.

Some whispered that Connor Grant was the finest swordsman in the land. Others insisted that honor belonged to his cousin Loki. Derric had never seen either man fight.

He lowered his weapon, nodding a greeting to Connor, and Alick turned to see what had caught his attention. "Uncle Connor," he said in greeting, and his uncle stepped forward and clasped his shoulder.

"Take a step back, Alick. I'd like to see if this man has any skills."

Alick provided an unnecessary introduction—"Derric, this is Dyna's sire, Connor Grant."

"Greetings to you, Laird Grant. My thanks for your hospitality. I don't plan to impose on it for long."

Connor Grant stepped closer to him, his keen eyes assessing everything he could in one look, if Derric were to guess. "You're welcome anytime. You brought my daughter home safely, and I know she can be a wee bit stubborn. With a fever, she's nearly unbearable. But we raised her to be a strong lass. My wife and I don't believe there's a difference between the strength of men and women."

Derric arched a brow at that statement. He wished to argue with him. After all, men were on average larger than women. Better swordsmen.

As if reading his mind, Connor said, "Physical strength isn't everything. We raised Dyna to be skilled in archery, and her mind is as keen as any man's."

"I'll not disagree with you there, Chief." She was smarter than most of the men he knew. "She's a talented lass."

"Spar with me, Corbett?"

"Aye." Doing his best to hide the sudden tremors shooting through him, he turned away, giving the man a chance to stretch his muscles. He'd heard once that older men had to be more careful about such things.

"Take the first swing, Corbett," Connor said, signaling he was ready.

Derric turned back to find the man staring at him intently with a narrowed gaze. It was intimidating enough to make him consider leaving, but he decided to stand tall and do his best. This was exactly the reason he'd been fighting and practicing with the Grant cousins.

Derric took a swing that Grant easily blocked, parrying it so powerfully it nearly sent him into the air. But he wouldn't give in so easily.

Many of the other men had stopped their own practicing to watch, but Connor ordered, "Keep them back, Alick. They're not to be close enough to overhear our conversation."

Alick followed his uncle's instructions, moving the onlookers back. Derric had an odd feeling that the chieftain was playing with him, just keeping the contest going until he had the chance to see if Derric had any skills at all.

This was a test.

He had every intention to rise to the occasion.

Next to Connor Grant, he had very little to offer, but he gave it his all, strictly because the man was Dyna's sire. He hated to admit it, but he wished to impress the man for Dyna's sake, and his sword skills were all he had to offer as proof of his worth. What more was there for a traveling camp follower of Robert the Bruce? You fought well or you weren't valued.

He'd parried with Alick for quite a while before taking on the chieftain, having no idea he'd be called to perform against the Grant, and his shoulders began to ache from the onslaught. He did his best to hide his pain, continuing to hold his own against the legendary swordsman opposite him.

They didn't battle for long before Connor let loose his strongest blows, driving Derric backward with the onslaught, barely able to stop the powerful thrusts until he tripped and fell on his backside, losing his grip on his sword and dropping it to the ground.

Connor Grant stood over him, settling the tip of his sword a bit away from his throat. He bent over Derric and said, "My thanks for bringing Dyna home, but you'd be wise to remember whose daughter you tarry with once she's hale."

Derric gave him a brief nod, trying not to focus on the sword point that was uncomfortably close to his throat. He'd been threatened by her cousins, her grandfather, and now her father.

He shouldn't be surprised, but he was. Connor tossed his sword to the ground, then offered him a boost to his feet, the man barely breathing any faster than he would be if he were eating his dinner. When Derric was standing in front of him, Connor asked, "Do you have any intentions toward my daughter?"

Derric lied his arse off and shook his head. "We're friends. I fought with the four cousins in Glasgow, and Els is married to my sister. 'Tis no more, no less."

Bloody hell, but he'd just lied to the toughest swordsman of all the Scots.

He was a dead man.

CHAPTER ELEVEN

LATER, DERRIC REQUESTED A VISIT with Dyna, and her mother escorted him up to see her. She did not move once the whole time he was there, although it was admittedly just a few minutes.

"I don't wish to disturb her," he said to Sela Grant, his eyes locked on Dyna's prone body, her even breathing telling him she was healing simply because it was calmer and more rhythmic than it had been the previous day. "You have spoken with her?"

"Aye, she's awakened. Actually ate porridge this morn, but her head was still paining her."

He stayed for a few minutes longer and then took his leave, fighting the urge to lean over and plant a soft kiss on her forehead. Her mother had said little, though her gaze had taken in everything he did. He knew where Dyna had gotten her willowy shape, her pale hair, and her ice blue eyes. She looked exactly like her mother. The sheer contrast of Connor, dark-haired and huge, and Sela Grant, willowy and white-haired, standing next to each other had to be arresting. He understood why they were leaders of their clan.

Last eve, Connor had given him leave to sleep in the chamber at the end of the great hall, apparently Alex Grant's chamber. Alick had led him to it the previous night, pointing to the small bed to the side rather than the behemoth in the center of the room. "This one's yours. No one sleeps in Grand-sire's bed."

He returned to the chamber and removed his tunic and his boots and fell onto the bed. The swordplay had exhausted him enough that he was asleep in seconds.

He only slept for half the night before he was awakened by a woman's wild screams. The tortur-ous sounds were so awful that he couldn't imagine what would have caused them. He ran into the great hall, expecting to see someone had fallen down the staircase or suffered some equally painful injury, but no one was there.

A lithe form flew down the staircase and then across the great hall. Dyna. He called out to her, but she ignored him, racing toward the tower.

He followed her up the twisting tower stairs, which ran around the edge of the tower in a cir-cular fashion, and through the first door on the second floor. She paused in the doorway of a pri-vate chamber. Although he stayed behind her, he could see her sister flailing wildly on a bed close to the door, her screams wild. Their mother sat in a chair across from her, kneading her hands while

Dyna reached for Claray and spoke to her in a soft voice. "There, there. I've killed them all. They'll not bother you again."

Connor came out from an attached chamber, wrapping his arms around Sela. "Another one so soon?"

"Aye," Sela replied. "I have no idea why they are starting up again. Dyna, you must go back to sleep or you'll get sick again. 'Tis why I didn't want you sleeping in the tower. How could you hear her?"

"I felt her screams, Mama," she said softly. "I didn't need to hear them." She started rocking her sister back and forth, singing softly. Her fingers ran through her sister's dark red waves, a soothing ministration that clearly calmed her.

Something softened inside of him. If this wasn't proof of a soft heart, he didn't know what else could be. Perhaps he'd just found the answer to part of his quest. Alex Grant would probably have seen this situation many times. The fact that no one else had come up to the tower at such a torturous sound indicated this was a common occurrence.

"Can I help?" he whispered, afraid to break the spell she had cast over her sister.

Dyna shook her head and waved him back out the door. He left, though he wished to speak with her. He wished to know what had happened to make her sister scream so. Dyna had said she'd killed them all. Killed what?

Back in the great hall, he grabbed an ale from a side table and took a seat in front of the hearth, the dying embers still crackling out enough heat to warm him.

A few moments later, Dyna entered the hall, coming over to take the chair next to him.

"She is better?" he asked, offering her an ale.

Dyna refused the ale, let out a deep sigh, and leaned over to rest her elbows on her knees. "Aye." He could hear a hitch at the edge of her voice, as if she were fighting tears. She stared at the floor as if embarrassed by her emotions.

"May I ask what caused it? What was she striking out at with her arms?"

Dyna sat back up, her battle with her emotions over, and said, "Spiders. She thinks she's killing spiders. Thinks they're attacking her."

"What? Why?" It wasn't until he asked that he remembered the conversation they'd had at MacLintock Castle. Els had said something about spiders, hadn't he?

"My mother was forced to work for an evil group of men. One of the ones who controlled her was a twisted person named Hord. He liked to collect spiders, and if Mama didn't follow their instructions, he would place her in a small chamber and unleash a bag of biting spiders."

"Bloody hell. But Claray?"

"My mother did something this Hord didn't like, and one day he sent Claray into the chamber with her. My sister was three. My mother still has nightmares about it occasionally. Claray seems to go in streaks. They're back again. She fights the spiders in her mind."

"So they were both bitten by this large horde of

spiders?"

"Aye. I try verra hard not to imagine it, lest I succumb to the fear myself. My father, grandfather, and grandmother rescued them from those bastards. Hord came back to kidnap Mama, and my father killed him."

"I'm sorry you all have to deal with such a thing." He glanced over at her, still beautiful even though she'd been sick for days. The longing to touch her, to hold her stole over him, but he fought it. "How do you feel? Better? You were quite sick in the cave."

"Aye, I'm not completely healed, but I feel much better. My thanks for getting me back here safely. I don't recall the ride home at all."

Derric snorted. "Because you slept through it. You leaned against me and didn't wake up until I carried you up the stairs to put you on the bed. Your mother took over then."

"When are you leaving?" She rubbed her hands together in front of the hearth.

"Probably on the morrow, or I may wait one more day. I have a favor to ask."

"Go ahead. If I can help, I will."

"I'm heading north to join Robert the Bruce's camp. I would like you to come with me. I think you'd be a big help to our cause, especially since we don't have many archers and the ones we have don't possess your skill."

She nodded slowly. "As soon as I'm well enough, I'd like to go on this mission with you." She glanced over at him then, rubbing her hands together. "I know something's coming—a battle—but I don't know where. I only know it won't happen here." Her gaze turned more intense, scrutinizing him. "I also know there's something you're not telling me."

"Aye." Damn if the lass wasn't too perceptive by half.

Unable to look her in the eyes, he stared at his own hands, flexing his knuckles. "Robert told me one of the camp followers I spent time with last year has a bairn. He wondered if the wee lass might be mine."

Dyna said nothing but arched a questioning brow at him.

"'Struth is I don't know. I did my best…" He cleared his throat, wondering how much detail to give an innocent like Dyna. "I tried not to father any bairns. But I intend to search her out to learn the truth of it. Robert told me Senga was in the north. I would like to meet up with her to see if 'tis possible I have fathered a bairn."

"And you're telling me all this why?" she asked, her voice hard. Not that he was surprised.

He stood and paced in front of the hearth. "I didn't wish to surprise you."

"And if you do have a daughter?" she asked, not looking at him.

"Then I'll offer her mother marriage. My sire taught me to be responsible." And because he wanted her to come with him, he added, "I invited you along because we could really use your fighting skills."

Dyna rubbed her hands together again and

said, "Derric, you've already made it clear you're not interested in me. Consider what's happened between us as curiosity on my part. There'll be no more of it. You may pursue whomever you like. Let me know exactly when you plan to leave to join the Bruce, but I need to go back to bed."

He sat down and said, "Dyna, you're wrong. How can you even think that after everything we've shared? I wish to clarify something. I am interested in you. Verra interested. Aye, I've had quick, meaningless relationships with women, but I've never been involved in something more serious. I'm not even sure how to go about this. Should I ask your father if I can pursue a relationship with you?"

"Why? You've already said you're not interested in marrying me."

"There is something between us. You cannot deny it any more than I can. At first, it was an experimentation or a tease, but you know it has become more than that. I wasn't ready to pledge to marry you when we first discussed it, but aye, I do want us to consider the possibility. Is it so wrong that I wish to take our time and get to know each other better before we become betrothed?"

"Many people are just told who they'll marry. There's no chance for consideration."

"Your parents were that way?"

She lifted her chin and stared at the far wall. "Nay."

"Then is that what you want—to be told who you can marry?"

"Nay, but I want you to be honest with me, and

I don't want you to feel forced into something because my clan has threatened you."

He wiped his hand down his face. He'd never felt so awkward, so foolish about a conversation. "Please help me. Will you answer one question for me?"

"If I can." Her pursed lips told him that he'd summoned her stubborn streak.

"Are you interested in me? In pursuing a relationship that could lead to marriage? May I court you?"

"We're not at court."

"I know that. But I thought that implied a certain level of interest. I don't know for sure how to ask, but I've spent all my adult years living with men in the forest, fighting for freedom. I'm not knowledgeable about some things. Please help me here a wee bit?" His voice came out a little louder than he'd anticipated, but she was not helping the situation. He stood up. "Never mind. I can see you're not interested in continuing this conversation. I accept your rejection."

He stood without looking at her and headed back toward Alex Grant's chamber. *What's done is done.* At least he knew where he stood now.

"Derric?"

He stopped but didn't turn around. "Aye?"

She came up behind him and took his hand. "I am interested in you."

With that short sentence, his entire world changed from frustration to hope. Turning, he caught her gaze and gave her a light kiss. "That pleases me. I hope you'll consider traveling with me. The only way we'll know for sure is to spend more time together. Away from here."

She smirked. "You mean without my threatening family watching our every move."

"Aye, but I can deal with that if I must. Think on it, please."

All Derric wished to do was take her to his bed and hold her. But he couldn't do that, not yet, so he settled for kissing the top of her head.

"We'll talk on the morrow," he said.

"Aye." She climbed the stairs, her head down.

This lass had far more depth than he'd realized. He could tell her grandsire that he'd met his quest and more.

Dyna Grant was a strong, fierce lass, and just as her grandsire had known, she also had a soft heart. He'd do whatever he could not to wound it.

CHAPTER TWELVE

DYNA FELL INTO BED, GRABBING a fur and burying herself under the covers. All of the turmoil she'd felt for the last several days had been for naught. Derric was interested in her, but if she had to guess, he wasn't going to make a commitment to her until he found out if he had a daughter somewhere.

She wished she had the nerve to ask him not to search Senga out. What if the lass was his? He'd said he wasn't interested in Senga, but if she was in a bad situation, Derric would probably insist on helping her out. Would he marry her to protect her?

It was cruel of her to even think about putting a halt to it, something most unlike her, but the thought of him marrying someone else made her feel like she'd been stabbed in the chest.

She buried her head under the covers. There was no reason to torture herself. She'd have her answer soon enough.

When she awakened the next morn, she felt more

like herself. This sickness had passed, although the strange feelings in her chest were worse than they'd been the night before. That would pass too—it would have to. She washed up and made her way down to the hall, only then realizing she'd missed the earliest group. It was several hours past dawn.

She'd slept longer than she'd thought.

Her mother and father sat talking at one of the trestle tables, their conversation stopping as soon as she hit the bottom step. "Greetings to you both. How is Claray?"

"She's fine," her mother said. "Barely remembers the nightmare. She's gone out to the gardens."

She went to the kitchens for some porridge and then returned to the hall to sit down with them, grabbing a hunk of brown bread from the loaf on the table.

"Trouble with your friend?" her father asked, arching a brow at her.

"What friend?" She didn't like the fact that her parents could see through her so easily.

"Derric. You are upset with him?" her mother asked, using that calm voice she usually reserved for Claray. It annoyed Dyna, and she stabbed at her porridge a little too aggressively—a mistake she regretted immediately.

Glancing up at her parents to see if they'd noticed, she found two sets of eyes upon her. "I'm not upset with Derric, I just didn't sleep well. I was hoping that Claray's nightmares wouldn't come back this time." She ate a glob of porridge and mumbled with her mouth full, "'Tis about time they stopped, do you not think?"

"You can move on with your life, daughter," her father said softly. "Claray will be fine if you marry someone."

She bolted out of her seat, her voice coming out in a strangled burst she barely recognized. "Who said I wished to marry anyone?"

Her mother reached across the table for her hand and gently pulled her back into her seat. "I didn't wish to acknowledge feelings for your sire either. Even then, I told myself I didn't care."

"Papa?" She stifled a snort. "But why? Didn't you love him right from the start?"

Her parents turned to stare at each other and burst into laughter.

"What does that mean?" She knew their relationship had been difficult at the start, especially because her mother had been controlled by those bastards, but why wouldn't she have wanted to get away?

Her father grinned. "The first time we met, on the docks in Inverness, we stood a hand's width apart assessing each other. Neither of us said a word, and when we did, 'twas not kind."

She set her utensil down, staring from one face to the other. "Truly?"

Her mother nodded, smirking as she reached for Connor's hand under the table. This was what Dyna wanted. A relationship like her parents' marriage. Fierce yet tender. "Your father didn't know I was working for those men against my will. He didn't know about Claray. He was quite harsh, and

I didn't know what to expect from him. I'd spent years around men who were motivated by personal gain, not honor. I struggled to understand his motivations. I struggled believing his actions were true and honorable. It was a foreign idea to me. Inconsistent with all the men I knew."

"Papa harsh? I do not believe you, Mama. How could you believe him harsh?" She took another bite of her porridge just because she didn't wish to appear too interested in these new details about their story. Secretly, she was awaiting every word.

"'Tis true. I hated him. Nay, I feared him." She studied her husband, assessing him as if they were both back in Inverness on the docks. "I was afraid to have any feelings for him because I feared he'd disappear and leave me."

Dyna wiped her mouth with a linen square, pondering this thought, something that resonated with her. She understood that fear because she worried Derric would just disappear, like he had so many times already.

"When did you meet Derric?" her mother asked. "How did the first encounter go?"

Dyna snorted, something she tried—belatedly—to cover with a linen square.

"That well, aye?" Papa asked.

"'Twas not the best. He insulted his own sister and I didn't like it. Joya is one of the most wonderful people I've ever met."

"You were upset with him…"

"Aye, Papa. He did anger me, so I reacted honestly and put him in his place."

"And his place was?"

"On the ground. I tripped him and set my knee upon him."

"So you were on top of Derric?" her mother asked, stifling a giggle.

Her parents exchanged a look again, and Dyna shoved aside what was left of her bowl of porridge, annoyed by their inquisition.

"It doesn't matter how we met, or what's happened since," she insisted. "There was nothing between us in the beginning, so I had no reason to handle him carefully." She scanned the hall to make sure no one else had entered. "He might have a daughter."

"And that matters why?" her father asked. "You remember your mother had a daughter when we met?"

"I'm aware of that, but if the lassie is his, Derric may decide to offer her mother marriage. He could choose her over me."

Her mother used that soft, comforting tone again. "And you'd prefer he desert his daughter and her mother? Have you asked Grandsire about this situation?"

But she didn't have time to answer, because her father had questions for her, too. "So he's not sure the bairn is his? Was the mother a camp follower, who..." He scowled, his hand scratching his jaw. "Never mind."

"Papa, I'm not a bairn," Dyna scoffed. "I understand the ways of men and women. So much so that I wish I didn't have this foolish piece of skin that everyone wishes to guard so well." That would surely put a halt to their conversation.

Or so she hoped.

Her mother patted her hand. "Don't give up on the man. He has true feelings for you, whether you see it or not. And I can see you care for him. If you did not, you would never have slept well in front of him on the horse. You trust him. 'Tis why we keep questioning you about your feelings."

She shrugged her shoulders, afraid her voice would give her away. The thought of putting her feelings for him into words frightened her. Somehow it would make them seem more real.

"You doubt us," her father said. He stood and held his hand out to her mother. "I think we can show you exactly how we were when we first met. What say you, Sela? Can you dredge up the feelings you once had? The feelings that took over on that dock in Inverness?"

Her mother stood, taking her father's hand. Dyna had no idea what they were about to do, but no one could have pulled her away from the spectacle in front of her. She was powerless, unable to avert her gaze, her eyes riveted on the couple who stood facing each other.

Her mother said, "I recall it verra well. My fear was that you would get me in trouble with my captors, that they would see you standing close to me and accuse me of causing the problem."

Her gaze changed to such a coldness that even Dyna was shocked to see.

Her father continued, "But I had no idea what

your life was like. Had I known about the bastards, I would have promised to rescue you. Instead, mayhap Hord ran through your mind. I'd been told you were called the Ice Queen, that you were as cold as anyone. That you had a reputation that preceded you." His gaze locked on his wife's.

Dyna couldn't believe the tension passing between them.

"We fought each other, denying the attraction," her mother said. "Because I was afraid of it. Of you." Her mother's gaze moved from her father to her, and she quickly blushed. "But I knew, in that moment, that my life would never be the same, yet I was afraid to see how it would change. Are you afraid of Derric for some reason, Dyna?"

She was, but she'd never admit it to her mother. Raging in her gut was a powerful fear that he would choose Senga over her. And if that happened after she'd admitted that she wanted him, that she might want to even *marry* him, she would look foolish to everyone.

Rejected.

She didn't say any of that, but somehow her mother knew anyway.

"You're being overdone," Sela said. "If he chooses to take responsibility for his daughter, it's not the same as rejecting you. You can't turn love off so easily."

She couldn't help but snort at the word love. While Derric had feelings for her, it wasn't love. Not yet.

But could it be? Could she hope they could

have a relationship like her parents? If theirs had started so poorly, could the same not be said of the relationship she had with Derric? It had definitely been rocky from the start.

Yet she couldn't walk away from him.

"And as for that piece of skin you mentioned earlier, you'll not hear me arguing with you. Do with it as you wish. 'Tis your choice. No one but you."

This time, she was left speechless.

Derric caught up with her that evening as she hurried outside, driven by a dream she'd had. She'd closed her eyes for a short while, exhausted from lack of sleep, and now sleep was the farthest thing from her mind. "Where are you headed?"

"I have a small archery field at the far end of the outer bailey."

"May I come along?"

"Of course. I need to see if I've lost any of my skills."

"You're too skilled to lose your abilities so quickly."

Should she tell him more about her premonition? About the new fears that had twined with the old?

"I hope you're correct." She glanced up at him and he smiled, that handsome smile that always sent a shiver through her.

He didn't mince words, putting his question to her directly. "Have you decided yet if you wish to travel with me?"

"I'm still considering it."

"The Bruce could use your help." He settled his hands on his hips, and it took all of her control not to wrap her arms around him and rest her head on his chest. Even now, she wished to touch him. To feel his heat. Because she sensed he struggled with his own feelings as much as she did with hers.

He didn't like not knowing if he had a bairn out there, and she sensed that part of the reason was because he *did* care about her. Mayhap it was time to end this situation. Mayhap she'd even help him find Senga, in the hopes that the bairn would prove not to be his daughter. Either way, all the dreams she was having pointed to being off Grant land.

"I'll go with you. I promised Grandsire I would keep him abreast of the Bruce's activities. Papa will send a score of guards to aid in any skirmish we meet along the way."

His shoulders dropped immediately. "Then we leave at first light."

She stopped to face him after leading him to an isolated spot where they wouldn't be overheard. "Derric, if I tell you something, can you promise not to tell my parents?" She'd decided not to tell them. For if she did, she would never be allowed to ride toward danger.

"Aye, I'll keep your secret. What is it?"

She cleared her throat and glanced back at the people meandering in the courtyard. "Tell no one."

"I promise. You're scaring me, Diamond. What

is it?" He stepped closer to her, something that would have made her step back from him a short time ago, but she held her position simply because she liked having him close.

"I fell asleep for a short nap and had a dream."

"Everyone has dreams. Doesn't mean it'll come true."

"These kind usually do come true. 'Twas one of my seer dreams."

Something flickered in his eyes. A memory perhaps. He'd seen enough to know her intuition bore weight. "And?"

"And I dreamed Grandsire was missing and I was traveling all over the Highlands looking for him."

"But you found him." It was a statement more than a question.

"I did. But I couldn't get to him. He was in an old cottage and I couldn't get inside."

"Diamond, if that comes true, and I have my doubts, I'm sure you'll be able to figure it out." He clasped both of her shoulders. "You'll save him."

"I couldn't. Someone else did."

"Who?"

"You."

CHAPTER THIRTEEN

THEY WERE ON THEIR SECOND day of travel and expected to come upon the king's camp soon. They hadn't come across many other travelers, but what few they'd seen had informed them well. Word was the English had already arrived and gone straight to Ross land, so they weren't expecting to see them. The Lowlanders hadn't been spotted at all, which meant they could be anywhere, but Derric wasn't worried about battling them.

They reached a small clearing, and Derric signaled that they could stop to see to their needs. Everyone dismounted, Dyna too. Derric returned to the clearing first and he watched as she made her way back to him. Her coloring was much better than it had been a few days ago. "Diamond, you are hale?"

She scowled as she stepped up to him. "Of course. Why wouldn't I be?"

He crossed his arms. "Because you were sick with a fever less than a sennight ago? Or were you so sickly that you forgot?"

She reached for his forearm and patted it. "I'm jesting with you. I feel fine and my thanks for asking. How much farther to the Bruce's camp?"

"We'll be there before dusk. It—" He stopped, silenced by the sight of a woman riding toward them on horseback. A woman all alone. She was too far away for him to see her well, but she had long, thick red hair. He walked away from Dyna, heading toward the lass because he had a funny suspicion it could be Senga.

"Is that her, Derric?" Dyna called out behind him, her voice thin.

He didn't answer her because he wasn't sure. Because his chest was suddenly filled with dread.

Dread that she was coming for him.

Dread he'd be forced to marry someone he didn't love.

Dread he was about to be dragged in five different directions.

He let his breath out in a loud whoosh as soon as he realized it wasn't Senga. His reaction had made something clear to him. Even if he had fathered Senga's bairn, he could not marry her. They were not suited at all.

The lass approached and said, "I'm looking for the Grants."

"These are the Grant warriors. What do you want?"

She stopped her horse in front of him. "I was sent from King Robert's camp. He heard there were Grants in the area and wishes for them to stop at his camp. I have guards to make sure I'm safe." She pointed off to a group of guards behind her, ones he'd never seen because his attention had been fixed on her.

"We are headed there. How much farther?"

"Less than an hour north and west of the main path. Head west after you pass the small village."

She left as quickly as she'd arrived. He couldn't move, thinking on all the emotion and the memories that the lass had brought out of him. A small voice carried to him from behind.

"Was that her? She has beautiful red hair."

"Nay, 'twas not. But she's from Robert's camp. He wants the Grant contingency to stop at his camp to update him on what's transpired."

"How did he know there was a Grant contingency?"

"Because King Robert knows all. He has patrols everywhere, as any good king would." He paused, then said, "For a moment, I did think 'twas Senga. Seeing her brought on a host of memories, and I feel I can tell you something now without any hesitation."

She took a step closer, her expression still wary, not that he blamed her. "What?"

He moved close enough that he could cup her face with one hand. "I cannot marry Senga."

"But if you have a daughter?"

"I'll offer Senga support, even invite them to live near me. Senga has no clan to my knowledge, so if she has a child, she's probably ready to give up following the camps. Mayhap I could convince her to settle in the same clan I join."

"And which clan will that be?"

"Diamond, if you don't know this by now, I'll be direct. I go wherever you go." He ran a thumb across her bottom lip. "Our time will come, lass."

A guard yelled to him, "Corbett, mind your hands. You're not to be touching the laird's daughter."

"Shut your mouth and mind your own business, Ewan." Dyna stepped around Derrick and pulled out her dagger.

Derric took her hand and pulled her back. "Diamond," he said with a wink when she finally looked at him. "He's doing his job." They moved back to their horses. He tossed her up onto her saddle and barked, "One hour north and we'll be at our destination."

They arrived before dusk, and King Robert himself greeted them, as was his custom. Once his guards cleared the new arrivals, he preferred to speak to them himself. "I'd heard of a Grant group not far away. Tell me if all is well."

"No problems yet, King Robert." Derric introduced Dyna to him.

"My lady," King Robert said. "I recall another time you aided our cause, and I'll thank you for it. Any Grant is welcome here."

"Do you have word of an attack yet?" Dyna asked. "We witnessed a cavalry of Englishmen headed north several days ago."

"Nay, we've heard naught, just that there are many after me. My intention is to send a message to Thane and Ross. And after William's treachery in turning my wife over to Edward, his day of reckoning is nigh. 'Tis time for him to pay for his betrayal. Poor Elizabeth has yet to be freed. Perhaps if we overtake Ross, Edward will get the message that we'll not go away anytime soon."

"When will you attack Thane?" she asked. Her interest was likely personal—her cousin Alick's wife was the niece of the clan chieftain.

"Not until I discover exactly where the English garrison is, though I suspect 'twill get cold enough for the English to retreat. They'll run from the cold weather. You'll see I'm right." He had a gleam in his eyes as he said it. They all enjoyed taunting the English, who lacked the constitution for winter in the Highlands.

Dyna nodded, then headed off into the woods to see to her needs, giving Derric the chance to question the king. "Senga, have you seen her?"

Robert's entire demeanor changed. "Lad, I fear I gave you poor information. Word reached me as soon as we arrived that Senga died over a moon ago from the fever. When I inquired about the bairn, I was told the lassie is with her sire, so apparently 'tis not you. I should never have said anything to you, but Senga is gone."

The news wrenched something inside of him. She'd been so young, so hale, and she'd left behind a wee babe. While he hadn't wished to marry her, he'd never wished for her to meet such a fate. He saw death all the time—it was a fact of war, of life—but this felt different. It felt wrong. He rubbed his whiskers, trying to tamp down the confusing surge of emotion. "The wee lass's father? She was certain 'twas his?"

"So she said. I was told the bairn's sire is Guinne. Earvin Guinne. The lass is with him, so best let it be."

"Where will I find Guinne?" He trusted Robert, but he couldn't rest easy about the situation until he saw the babe with his own eyes. He wondered if Dyna would go with him, though he wouldn't question her if she refused.

"He's headed west." He deliberately changed the subject rather than give Derric more specific directions. "Though I could use your talents here. I've arrived at a truce with Macdougall, and now I'm off toward Ross land. I know not what we'll face, especially if they've brought other Lowlanders in to fight, but I'll not shy from the challenge." He paused, studying Derric. "You have about a short time before we ride. Make your mind up." Then the King of the Scots spun on his heel and left.

Derric turned around, watching Dyna's regal carriage take her across the group of men, heading back into camp from the woods. Every man turned to look at her, and he wished to break every one of their necks for staring at her so.

Mine.

He knew it wasn't true, but he *wished* it were. Still, she was such a powerful force of nature, he didn't know if he was capable of reining her in.

Dyna would balk at that statement. She would say she didn't need reining in, and he'd be forced to agree with her. The lass didn't need changing. She was remarkable as she was. She was one of a kind.

"Is she here?" Dyna asked on her approach, her hands on her curvaceous hips.

"Nay," he said. "She died of fever."

Dyna's eyes widened. She reached out to touch him, her fingers wrapping around his forearm, sending flames through him even through his thick tunic. "Derric, I'm so sorry." She leaned toward him and gave him a quick hug. "I know 'tis not what you wanted."

"Aye, I'm sorry it happened, but the loss isn't mine. We were...it wasn't like that between us. I meant what I said a short time ago. We were not meant to be together. Robert says the lassie isn't my daughter, that she's with her father."

"And how do you feel about that?"

He wasn't sure. "Does it sound daft if I say I wish to see her for myself? I want to know she's well cared for."

"Aye, and 'twill help you decide whether there's a chance you're her sire. Most lads and lassies look like one parent or another. If she looks like Senga, you may not be sure, but if she looks like her father and nothing like you, it could ease your worry."

He paced in a small circle. "Aye, what you say is true. I think I must see for myself. Would you care to travel with me? 'Tis west of here."

"Nay," she said, staring at her boot as she kicked a stone about in the dirt. "You must do this on your own. I'll be here when you return."

He nodded and leaned in to plant a kiss on her

forehead. "I'll be back shortly." He left her and headed into the woods to take care of his needs. In truth, he also needed a moment to think on what he'd just learned. On Senga's death.

When he finished, he walked over to the nearby burn and rinsed his hands, throwing water on his face to wash away the grime of travel.

A sense of guilt rooted in him as he washed. Part of him felt he should be sadder, that he should mourn Senga more deeply. The sadness he felt was for a life lost too soon, not for what might have been.

Having faced up to the possibility of losing Dyna, he knew the only future he wanted was with *her*. His feelings for her were real, and they were strong. If the fever had taken her, he would have raged at the world. He would have torn it apart.

Mayhap he was finally experiencing that emotion that had proven so elusive to him.

Love.

It was something he'd never felt for anyone besides his sister and his parents, and until recently, he'd been parted from all of them for so long that he'd almost forgotten what it felt like.

He'd spent all this time fighting for his country, but he'd almost forgotten why he was fighting. Part of him wanted to belong to a clan—to be a part of the country he was protecting.

And he wanted that clan to be Clan Grant.

He stood, then folded his hands in front of him and said a brief prayer to God for Senga, expressing his hope that she'd be accepted into heaven, his sorrow that she'd been taken too soon, and his shame for not having loved her like he should.

He cupped water and tossed it over his hair, running his hands through the thick locks to try to straighten what he could, but a sound interrupted him—Dyna's voice—and the words she said ripped his insides out.

"Take your hands from me."

He couldn't see her, but he heard her voice as clearly as if she stood next to him. Racing out of the woods, he didn't have to look far before he found her in the middle of a few warriors. One had his hand on her shoulder and the other had his hand on her arse.

He roared and charged toward them, pounding his fist into the first man's face. "Leave her be!" He noticed three Grant guards coming to her rescue as well. But they stood back, waiting to see what would happen next.

"Derric, stand down. I can protect myself," Dyna said, her voice seething. She had the second man in a headlock, and he watched as she twisted him to the ground and put her knee to his chest, bringing her dagger to his throat.

Someone must have summoned King Robert, or else he'd heard the noise, because he hurried toward them bellowing, "There'll be no killing. I need these men."

But Derric was in a fury, and even his king's remark couldn't stop him. "They touched her and they had no right," he growled, blocking a retaliatory punch from the first man and slamming him to the ground. He punched him twice, once in the belly and again in the face, then spun around to handle the second man.

There was no need. Dyna still had her dagger at his throat.

"Touch me again, and I'll cut your sacs while you sleep." The man didn't say a word, only gave her a brief nod of agreement. She kneed him lightly in the groin before she stepped away, sheathing her knife. "I don't need your help, Corbett," she snapped.

"Are we done with the fighting?" Robert asked.

Derric wiped a hand across his mouth and muttered, "Aye, I'm finished. But tell your men that she's off limits."

"'Tis her choice, Corbett, not yours."

"I'm not interested in anyone here," Dyna clarified. "They can all keep their hands to themselves. That includes you, Derric."

She strode away without another word, and the rest of the group scattered except for Robert. The king clapped him on the back. "She's not welcoming your advances? Is that what has you strung up? If I hadn't known better, I'd have guessed the lass had you by the bollocks, not Struan. Sorry I didn't introduce you to some of my new men. Struan is a fine fighter, so please leave him be."

"Aye, I'm interested in her," he admitted. "But I didn't know what the situation was with Senga and the lassie. It left me a bit confused."

King Robert's brow furrowed, his expression telling Derric in no uncertain terms what he thought of his explanation. "Why are you still concerned about the bairn? 'Tis as I said, she's been claimed by her father."

He shrugged his shoulders, unable to explain his reasoning other than with simple words. "I have to know."

"Fine," the king said with a brusque nod. "Guinne lives in the next village with her—less than an hour west. He was a warrior of mine, a good man. Once you see the two of them together, you'll not question what I told you."

"Why?"

"Son, you need to see with your own eyes. The next village. Guinne lives with his mother in the last hut. Farthest from the well. But please don't bother them."

He wiped the sweat from his face and knew he had to go. He'd talk to Dyna when he returned.

He had to see if he had a daughter.

CHAPTER FOURTEEN

DYNA STARTED PACING, TRYING TO process all that had transpired. Derric's irritating possessiveness. Senga's death. The possibility that he might still have a child out there.

The dream about Grandsire.

She closed her eyes and massaged her temples, wishing that small action could squeeze out another dream, another vision of the future. Of course it did not. She made a silent plea to the heavens to help her.

Still naught.

The dream haunted her. The worst part had been the feeling of helplessness, the knowledge that only Derric would be able to reach Grandsire. That she would not be able to do anything for either of them. Desperate to get the troubling images out of her mind, she only came up with one thought to distract her.

Derric with his tunic off.

She was still thinking about it, her mind summoning those hard ridges of muscle, when the very man she was imagining approached her from behind, making her jump. "Dammit, you could have warned me."

"Sorry, Diamond. I'm about to ride west, but I should be back in a couple of hours.

She nodded. "Godspeed. I'll be here."

Unable to tear her gaze from him, she watched as he hopped on his horse and left, speaking to no one else. He did look back once, winked at her, then went on his way. She'd do as he asked and wait for him. But she was starting to feel a desperate need for word about her dear grandfather.

A small group of horses approached the camp, and her eyes caught the familiar colors of their plaids. Grant warriors. She hurried over to where the other Grant guards had gathered, and together they awaited the arrival of the newcomers.

Her heart hammered in her chest as they waited. This new group had to be bearing a message.

"What is it?" she bellowed, not wishing to wait any longer.

She noticed that King Robert had joined them and was watching with interest.

The lead horse slowed, the horse foaming a little at the mouth from having been pushed too hard. The warrior jumped down and said, "I bear a message for you, Dyna, from your sire. You're needed at home."

She spun around, ready to find her horse and mount up, but Robert's question gave her pause. "Why? Is there trouble with the English?"

"We were not told, my king. We were instructed

to fetch Dyna only and escort her home."

King Robert stared at the man, a look that usually yielded results, she was sure, but the messenger said no more. The king finally nodded. "Grab yourselves an ale and water your horses at the burn before you leave."

The men dismounted, but one of them said, "We leave for the return trip in a quarter hour."

The king approached her. "If this involves another kidnapping of one of your clan," he said in an undertone, "I wish to be apprised of the matter immediately."

He was fully aware of all that had happened to their clan—to wee John, to Kyla, to Alex Grant—and if the English were to succeed in convincing the Grant lairds to use their warriors against Robert, it would effectively crush his efforts. Of course, her clan would never agree to that, but she couldn't fault him for his concern.

"I promise to send a messenger if so," she said. "How far away is Corbett? I expect he'll stay with you, but will you tell him where I've gone, if you please?"

"I will. He'll return by high sun." Something flickered in his eyes, and he added, "I'll make sure he gets your message."

The King of the Scots said no more, and she didn't dare push the man.

She moved to the burn to fill her skin, then mounted her horse, motioning for the nearly twenty Grant guards to follow. She only posed one more question to the new arrivals. "And this message was from my sire, correct? Not from my grandsire?"

"Aye, my lady," the leader said. "Connor Grant sent me. Alexander Grant has not returned from Cameron land."

That decided things. Her intuition told her this was about her grandfather. She'd be a wreck until she found out he was hale. Although she wished Derric would go with her, she could not wait for him to return.

Derric didn't have any trouble finding the village. He intended to keep his word to King Robert—he wasn't about to ask Guinne directly about the child's parentage—but he also didn't want to hide around the outside of the village as if he were a spy. He strode into the middle of a group of lasses talking near a well.

"I'm looking for Guinne."

The lasses looked him up and down, taking his measure, but one of them finally pointed to the last cottage, the one farthest away from the well, just as Robert had advised him. Only now he wouldn't need to explain how he knew.

He strode down the beaten path, attracting the notice of many curious onlookers, but no one stopped him. Before he could approach the door and knock, a man stepped out of the cottage. He carried an empty bucket, but he stopped to appraise Derric. "Do I know you?"

"Are you Guinne? Heard you'd traveled with

King Robert's warriors. I was wondering if you could tell me where to find them." He did his best to look innocent, but he was paying close attention to the man who'd caught Senga's eye.

Guinne was average height, stocky, but his weight was more from muscle than flab. His hair and full beard were both the color of the first carrot in summer, still young and bright. His skin bore the freckles common to redheads.

A loud cry came from inside the cottage. He shook his head and broke into a crooked grin. "We woke up the bairn, and she's got a fierce belly on her."

Derric didn't say a word, waiting for the man to go inside and check on the wee one, Senga's daughter. The man remerged into the gray day with his bucket, this time with a bairn strapped to his chest, the wee lassie's chubby face staring out at Derric.

She had a shock of carrot hair that perfectly matched her father's, and she grinned up at Derric as if she'd known him forever. She looked exactly like her sire, the hair, the skin coloring, even the smile. For a moment, he was at a loss for words. "Cute. What's her name?"

The man ran his hand across the top of her head, smoothing the red curls down as the bairn kicked her legs and swung her arms wildly. "Senga. I named her for her mother, God rest her soul. You going to fight for the Scots? You ever fight with him before?"

"Aye, I've traveled with him for many moons, off

and on. When were you there?"

"Not long. I fought with him for about a moon before I was called away. I'd fight with him now, but for this wee lassie. Her mother passed, and I'm the only one she has left. Once spring comes around and she's a bit older, we'll join my clan in the Lowlands. If you see King Robert, send him my best. He's a fair man, a hard-working man, and I surely hope he achieves his goals."

Derric nodded, looking at the bairn, her wide smile and green eyes glittering with glee. "I'm off to look for him now."

The lass opened her mouth and let out a roar, as if to tell her father she'd run out of patience. "Sorry I can't be of more help," the man said with a chuckle. "Got to get some goat's milk for the wee lass. Godspeed to you and all of the Scots."

Derric nodded and left, striding away with purpose.

Now he understood why King Robert had told him that he needed to set eyes on the wee bairn for himself. Senga had been yellow-haired, her locks even lighter than his own, with dancing green eyes that she'd given to her daughter.

That orange-red hair hadn't come from him.

Not a person in the world would believe the bairn belonged to Derric instead of Guinne.

Derric had no claim on her.

CHAPTER FIFTEEN

WHEN DYNA ARRIVED AT CLAN Grant, she could tell something had, indeed, happened. She saw it in the tension in the stable lads' shoulders as they saw to their horses. She saw it as she walked through the courtyard, passing several people who were working hard but silently. Clan Grant was usually a happy place, for the lairds provided for and cared for everyone.

She flung the door open with a huff and stepped into the great hall, waiting for her eyes to adjust to the darkness. Claray's voice rang out. "Dyna, thank goodness you're home. You won't believe all that has happened."

"Claray! Hold your tongue," her mother called out.

She made her way over to the crowded trestle table, where her mother and Claray sat with Aunt Kyla, Chrissa, Alick, and Branwen. "What happened?"

Her mother glanced at the others, then said, "Grandsire only spent one night on Cameron land.

He left the next day and hasn't been seen since."

Dyna lowered herself onto a nearby stool. "I knew something had happened. I knew it." Her hands played with her plait as she stared at her family. Should she reveal her dream to them?

Her mother gave her that look she hated, the one that was so intense she had a difficult time lying. "Another seer's dream?"

"Aye, Mama." She framed her face with both hands, then brought her fingers up to her hairline, attempting to smooth everything back after the windy ride. "I dreamed Grandsire was gone. He was in a cottage somewhere."

"Where exactly?" Aunt Kyla nudged.

"I don't know," she said, placing her hands on the table, forcing them flat so she'd stop fussing. "I've tried to pin it down, any details at all, but I keep coming up empty. I only know he'll be at a cottage."

"Is he being held captive?" Kyla persisted.

"Aye, he's sleeping, and I sense he's a prisoner, but I don't see anyone else in the cottage and I can't determine where he is exactly."

"Papa went after him," Claray declared, glancing at their mother.

"Your father went to Cameron land to speak with Aunt Jennie. See what she knows. He took a score of guards, and they plan on tracking him."

Dyna's head fell into her hands. She was so tired she could barely keep her head up. She needed sleep desperately, but she had to go after her grandfather. Her premonitions were usually stronger when she was physically closer to the person—or place—involved. Perhaps she should try to find him on her own.

Alick said, "I know what you're thinking and you're not going after him alone. I sent a messenger to MacLintock land. I'm sure Alasdair and Els will join us as fast as they can. You know as well as anyone that the four of us are more powerful together."

"When you go after Grandsire, I'm going with you," Chrissa declared with an emphatic toss of her plait over her shoulder.

Aunt Kyla stood up so quickly her chair nearly toppled over. "No one is going anywhere until Connor returns or we receive a message telling us what's going on. Chrissa, do not plan any more of your trickery around me."

Chrissa had snuck away from Grant land on more than one occasion. She'd become skilled at archery, so she was definitely an asset, but at two and ten, she was also capricious and unreliable. Chrissa cast Dyna a side glance as if to tell her she'd go with her. Dyna glanced at Aunt Kyla to see if she'd picked up on her daughter's intent, but she saw no sign of it.

"Now may I tell her my troubles, Mama?" Claray asked their mother, her eyes wide.

Sela nodded. "Aye, go ahead and tell your sister."

Claray was more fearful than most owing to her past, and Dyna had promised herself that she would always listen to her, even when her own mind was uneasy. "Tell me."

"Someone has been watching me," she whispered.

"Claray, we've kept the gates locked at all times ever since Mama was taken. 'Tis most impossible for you to have been watched by a stranger."

Her sister shook her head. "When we went out for a ride, someone was in the woods watching me. But the guards couldn't find him. He'd disappeared." Her voice cracked, indicating tears would be imminent.

"I'm going to take a short nap because I'm exhausted, but then I promise to look for this alleged stalker. If he's out there, I'll find him. Do you trust me, Claray?"

She nodded emphatically, a smile bursting across her face. Claray was so beautiful and sweet, yet her past held her back. It held her mind captive. "Promise, Dyna?" she asked softly.

"I promise. But first I must rest my eyes." She got off her stool, but before she left, she wrapped her arms around her sister. "Why don't you play with the younger ones?"

They had a younger brother and sister, Hagen and Astra. Hagen was the elder at four and ten winters. He was often with their father, but in Connor's absence, both of them would be with the group of bairns that played behind the castle while the clan worked at their chores. With all the attacks on the Grant family, Sela didn't allow their children outside the gates, even to the lists. Only Dyna.

"All right. Please don't rest for long, Dyna. I need you."

Sela patted Claray on the back and ushered her outside.

As soon as they were gone, Aunt Kyla gave Dyna a grim smile. "There's been no evidence of anyone watching her. We all suspect she's upset with both you and your father gone. She'll feel better now that she's seen you. Go rest. You look exhausted. When you awaken, you can tell us about King Robert."

Alick said, "Mayhap Alasdair and Els will be here by then. My guess is Emmalin and Joya will be here, too. And when your father returns, you know we'll be leaving soon after. You need sleep first."

She felt a pang at the mention of Joya, for it reminded her of Derric…and the fact that she'd left him without a word. Would she ever see him again?

But she didn't want to burden Aunt Kyla with her tribulations.

"There's not much to tell about King Robert," she said. "We met up with him in the north, but he came to a truce with Macdougall, so he didn't expect to go to battle imminently. He was going to see if Ross and Thane will support him, or if he needs to go to battle. You know how he feels about Ross."

"Ross betrayed him. He'll never forgive him for causing his wife to be turned over to King Edward. He'll make him pay. King Robert may overlook many things, but not that. You go rest for now."

Dyna nodded and climbed the stairs to her chamber, wishing that when she awakened, her grandsire would be sitting in front of the hearth.

Just like he used to do.

Derric made his way back to King Robert's camp, searching the area for Dyna, but there was no sign of her. Could she have left without him?

King Robert greeted him. "Did you find Guinne?"

"Aye, he was exactly where you told me he would be, and now I understand why you wished for me to see the lassie with my own eyes. She's Guinne's daughter, no doubt about it. He will take good care of her."

The king nodded. "You needed to see it for yourself. I suppose you are looking for the Grant contingency. They sent a messenger ordering Dyna back to Grant land at once."

"Why?" he asked, feeling the press of worry and a strange hollowness from the knowledge that she was no longer there.

"They wouldn't share that information, but she left right away. A rumor came in less than an hour ago that Alex Grant is missing. They suspect he's been taken by King Edward's men. He's probably being taken to Berwick by that English garrison. Might be why we've seen no sign of them in the north."

"Bloody hell, I'm going to Grant land. They'll need help."

"I'll send you along with only one message. God-speed and don't let the English win. I'm counting on the Grants to get him back. If Alex Grant makes it to Berwick, his head will be on a pike in no time. And that's if they don't attempt to use him first to move the Grant warriors against us."

Derric mounted his horse and bolted toward Grant land.

When Dyna awakened, she sat on the edge of her bed and made her plan. She needed to find out what had transpired while she was asleep, and if nothing had significantly changed, she would leave to find Grandsire on her own.

Dyna Grant was not the type of person who stood around and waited for things to happen.

She made them happen.

She stepped into the hall and quickly found a serving lass. "Fiona, would you send Claray up with a bowl of porridge, please? I'm hungry, but I need to wash up first. She can find me in Grand-mama's bathing chamber."

Fiona hurried away, and Dyna made her way to the chamber down the passageway, deep in thought. Her grandsire had been so in love with his wife that he'd built a special chamber for her because she liked to bathe so much. Of course, the guards liked to say it was because every time Mad-die went to the outdoor building that used to be used for bathing, forty guards fought to try to get a peek at the beautiful woman, but Dyna believed he'd done it out of love.

That was her vision of happiness in marriage.

The kind of love her grandfather and grandmother had shared, and the kind of love her parents still had for each other.

Would Derric build her a bathing chamber in their castle?

She snorted, quite unladylike, at the thought.

Claray entered the chamber a few moments later. "Dyna, will you go find the stalker? He was watching me when we were in the back last eve. He must have climbed a tree behind the curtain wall—I could feel him watching me. Mama sent the guards to check, but he was gone. I know he was there! No one else believes me, but I knew you would, Dyna. You must help. He frightens me."

"I promise to go looking for him."

Claray's eyes brightened. "Here's your porridge. I'll get you more if you need it."

"Nay, this is plenty. I'm going to bathe, and then I'll go look for your stalker."

Dyna didn't expect to find anything, but she'd promised. And she couldn't leave to look for Grandsire until she talked to someone. Learned what was known.

Could she?

CHAPTER SIXTEEN

ALEXANDER GRANT STOOD IN THE middle of the forest, talking to the person whose assistance he'd sought.

"Are you sure about this?" the other asked.

"Aye. I aim to put an end to this. They stole my grandson, my daughter, and they've put my family through hell trying to get to me. DeFry and Busby came to MacLintock land and said Edward's son will not stop until he has my head."

"You think giving him what he wants is the answer?"

"I've lived a full life. I'll not have a young life lost over my old one. This must end now. I had to choose carefully, but I've known you for many years. I believe you will assist me in this endeavor. I only have one caveat."

"And what is that?"

"You must tell no one. Will you agree?"

The man who stood in front of him thought carefully, something he should do. He knew what this action would bring down upon him. All the

Grants would come for him if they learned the truth.

But Alex trusted this man, trusted him with his life. He would do the right thing.

The man turned to him and clasped his shoulder.

"Aye, I'll assist you. Whatever it takes. I owe you much."

Alex Grant smiled and let out the breath he'd been holding.

This would end now.

CHAPTER SEVENTEEN

DYNA SNUCK OUT THROUGH THE side of the curtain wall, climbing a tree and dropping down to the ground. If she'd gone out the main entrance, she'd have been forced to bring guards along, and they moved as quietly as ten wolfhounds on the great hall. The only chance she had of catching the culprit was to sneak out on her own and catch the bastard unaware.

She'd have no trouble finding a horse since the overflow Grant horses were kept outside the gates. The stable lads watched them, but she was quick enough to get past without being seen.

She did as she promised and searched the area Claray had referred to, and to her surprise, she did find footprints, evidence of one man in the area. Still, the footprint could have been left by anyone, and Claray's fears were known by everyone in the clan. It likely meant nothing.

Ready to give up, she found a log and mounted her horse—she'd followed a hunch and taken her stallion rather than Misty—which was when a waking premonition stole over her.

Her grandfather stood talking to a man with no face. She tried to lock on to details from their surroundings but she couldn't. The two men stood in a forest, a castle in the distance, but there were no distinguishing characteristics at all. Who was that man?

They carried on a conversation that she couldn't comprehend until her grandsire smiled and said his last sentence as clearly as any she'd ever heard. "I'm handing myself over to the English so they'll stop bothering my clan."

A chill shot down her back, her body shivering in reaction to his comment. Could it be true? Would he be so foolish? She tried yelling at him, but the vision disappeared as soon as she spoke.

Dyna had meant to return to talk to the guards about the footprints. To see what was being done about Grandsire this morn. To elicit help from others in her clan. But the urgency of the vision caught hold of her and she rode off, away from Grant land, hoping that her guardian angel, or anyone, would lead her to her grandsire.

Flying across the landscape, her plait bouncing on her back, she smiled at the breeze in her face, the scent of the pines pleasing her as always. Was there a better scent in the world? Confident this was a sign of which direction she should go, she allowed herself the small luxury of basking in the beauty of the landscape.

But the feeling didn't last long. The heaviness of her grandfather's disappearance weighed on her.

It didn't make sense. Aedan Cameron himself had been with Grandsire. How could he have left soon? He'd been looking forward to spending time with his sister. Their relationship was so close, more like father and daughter than brother and sister, and she knew walking away from Jennie must have been difficult for him. Where had he gone?

Was the vision trying to tell her something else? Was Grandsire already with the English? But if so, wouldn't they be flaunting their good fortune for all to hear? Hell, they'd be spreading the word that his beheading would be coming soon.

The thought made her quite ill, but it also convinced her that he wasn't with the English yet. If he were, they would all know it.

So where was the crafty old man?

He'd had a group of Grant guards with him. Had it been five or eight? She couldn't recall, but if he'd been kidnapped, they'd be lying dead somewhere.

Her father had ridden to Cameron land to get the details, so she needn't do that. Instead, she rode down the most traveled road between the two places, searching for any signs of the Grant guards, a skirmish, or anything else that could help her find her grandfather. Even at his advanced age, he was still a hell of a swordsman, so if someone had kidnapped or tried to hurt him, they wouldn't have found it easy.

Hour after hour she traveled, stopping to study the brush or searching for evidence of traveling horses. Most of her time was spent cursing because she was so unsuccessful.

She couldn't find Claray's stalker, and she couldn't find her grandfather. Part of her had hoped she might run into her sire, that he would have good news to share or an idea of where his father had gone, but it hadn't happened. She'd be sleeping alone this night, something she wished she'd given more thought to when she'd galloped across Grant land with no destination in mind. Although she prided herself on her keen mind, sometimes her impulsivity put her in danger, or so her sire had always said.

She didn't feel safe at the moment.

Dusk was nearly upon her when she decided to find a cave for shelter. She knew of one not far ahead, so she made her plan to stop there. On the morrow she'd return to Grant land using the unpopular trails, hoping to unearth some clue to the location of her grandsire. And if she and her sire crossed paths along the way, she'd be pleased.

She hadn't gone far when her horse's ears perked up, so she slowed to see if anyone was within sight. Up until now, she'd been fortunate enough not to run into any reivers, but the danger was undeniable.

The distant sound of a single horse's hooves finally caught her ears, so she found a spot off the path and hid her horse to the side to allow the rider to pass. This was exactly the kind of situation her sire would rail at her for, being alone with no guards to protect her.

She'd pay the price later, but she had to find her grandfather. Then they could all yell at her as much as they wished.

What if it was too late? What if Grandsire was lying dead somewhere? What if he'd been robbed and beaten by reivers, and they'd left him to find his way back without a horse? He wasn't as strong as when he was younger. She fought the desire to panic. Her horse snorted as if to remind her they had more important issues at hand.

They could be facing a brutal attacker.

Holding her breath, she waited for the horse to pass. Quite certain it was only one horse, she readied her bow just in case she needed to attack.

To her complete surprise, the rider was someone she knew. Derric Corbett flew past, but then he stopped, almost as if he'd caught her scent. She brought her horse out into his view and

Derric dismounted immediately, tossing the reins over a bush and running toward her. "What the bloody hell are you doing out here alone, Diamond? I traveled to Grant land to find you, only to discover you'd run off brazenly on your own. Your clan is searching for you everywhere."

She reacted the only way she could. Jumping from her horse, she ran straight into his arms, and his lips found hers before she could answer. His heat warmed her and she tugged him back into the woods, away from the view of anyone who came along. His lips descended on hers and she moaned, not caring if he heard her. How she needed him right now. She needed him to make everything better.

He angled his mouth over hers, and their tongues

dueled in a savage dance she wanted everywhere. Before she knew it, she was tugging at his tunic, yanking it up over his arms and his head, her hands landing on his bare chest as soon as she tossed it aside.

"Just say aye, Diamond. Tell me you want this as much as I do," he whispered, pulling her tunic over her head, grasping at the binding around her chest and tearing at the rough cloth. When the mounds fell into his hands, she moaned again, his thumbs teasing her nipples to a hardness that she liked even more.

"Aye, please. I need you, Derric. I need *us*, please." What had possessed her to say such things? She didn't need him.

Did she? Before she knew it, she was lying on top of her own leggings, and he was doing things to her that would drive her to madness, she was sure of it. "Derric, please finish this. I need…" His hands caressed her bare bottom and she arched against him until his mouth descended on her nipple, suckling her until she tugged his hair. "More, I need more."

"You must promise me."

"Aye, aye, I promise."

"Diamond," he said, his hands stopping his caresses and coming up to cup her face. "Dyna, I mean it. Promise me you'll marry me if you become with child. Promise me. I'll not have my bairn growing up without a father."

"Aye. I'll marry you. Mayhap I'll even try to fall for you, but not unless you finish this."

He grinned at that declaration, and she nipped his shoulder. "Diamond, if I'm ever going to fall in love, it'll be with you and only you."

He kissed her again, this time tenderly, working her into a feverish pitch that she couldn't control. She begged him again. "Finish."

He spread her legs and settled himself between her thighs, his hand reaching for her sex, touching and caressing her until she wanted to scream. She moved against him and spread her legs even wider. It felt so good, so damn good. "Derric…"

She felt like she was on the precipice of the release she wanted, needed, and then he whispered, "I'm sorry."

He thrust inside of her and searing pain grabbed hold of her. "Derric, stop!"

"Diamond, it will only hurt for a minute or two," he said, pulling out. "I promise you'll like it again. I'll make you beg me again. Trust me."

A bolt of lightning and a crack of thunder interrupted them. It felt like a sign, and she shoved against him, rolling away, and reached for her leggings, stopping when she saw the blood on her thighs. Derric came up behind her and wrapped his arms around her.

"Dyna, I'm sorry, but didn't anyone tell you it would hurt the first time? That you would bleed? It won't last long."

"I know it won't last long because you're done. Get away from me. You set me up. It hurt terribly."

"It's not supposed to hurt that badly. It will go away. Give us a chance. Please."

Hellfire, but she wouldn't.

She was never having intimate relations with a man again. Emmalin and Joya were both daft. She hated lovemaking.

Alex Grant rode to his destination with the man he'd chosen to assist him. They were about two hours away when the skies opened up. A thick grove of pines was nearby, and they raced under the trees as fast as they could. His partner pointed to a large overhang where they could hide from the storm, an outcropping large enough for three men and their mounts.

The sky turned black, thunder clouds rolling in every direction.

The other man asked, "Have you ever seen clouds like that before? They're going in opposite directions, something I've not witnessed."

Alex got his horse under the stone protection and dismounted, patting Midnight down to console him. Although he was stalwart and footsure in battle, the beast had always reacted badly to thunderstorms, the quaking of the ground too much for him. He whispered sweet words to the animal and pulled out an apple from his saddlebag. The horse took it quickly and munched away, the treat calming him for a wee bit.

Alex set his hands on his hips, staring up at the thunderstorm raging around them. "I have seen one storm like this, and it was not from anything good. It meant evil was trying to steal a sapphire sword belonging to the fae."

"When did it happen?" the other man asked.

"Avelina Ramsay had control of the sword. She fought with a daft man over it. Her brother told me the storm started because she held the sword overhead. She was driving a man with ill intent away from her. I've never seen another sight like it. Howbeit…" He couldn't help but think of his granddaughter, Dyna. Blessed with the talents of a seer and the odd ability to pull power into her cousins' swords by holding her bow over her head, he began to see a similarity between her talents and those of Avelina Ramsay. Was there more to the spectral swords than he realized? And what part was Dyna playing in this unnatural storm?

He wondered where she was and who was with her. Then another thought thrust itself into his mind. The sapphire sword. His sister Brenna had said something about a challenge arising every fifty years. Their mother had told Brenna and Jennie about it, about how a fae queen would choose a mortal being when necessary to help save the Scots, but only when all else had failed.

He pushed his memory back to it, trying to remember all he'd learned, how Brenna had told him that Gregor had been near death, but that Avelina had held him and breathed life back into him.

The fae had given her special powers along with the sword. Avelina had fought against evil and won, and the fae queen had told her to hide the sword, that she would return when it was needed again. That was it. The fae queen had said there would be peace for a time, but eventually they would need to fight evil in Scotland again.

Was the time nigh?

"I wonder. Has it been fifty years?" He said it loud enough to be heard, though he hadn't meant to because anyone who heard him was bound to think him daft.

Then he shook his head, chastising himself for seeing things that weren't there. Besides, it couldn't have been more than forty years.

"What is it?" his companion asked.

"Naught," Alex replied. "Musings of an old man, one who wishes to believe his wife comes to him in his dreams and his grandchildren have special talents."

"Like an orphan dreams of being adopted some-day?"

Alex glanced at him and grinned. "Something like that."

The two men watched the wild gusting of the wind, the sheeting rain drenching the landscape, the thunder coming so quickly it was impossible to anticipate the claps.

Alex whispered to himself, "Never seen another like it until now."

The other man stared at him.

"And I don't like it."

CHAPTER EIGHTEEN

D ERRIC CUPPED HIS HANDS TOGETHER to catch enough rain to give Dyna water to wash the blood from her thighs. "Diamond, I'm sorry. I thought 'twas what you wanted. I'll marry you as soon as we find a priest. We'll suit each other. You'll see. You're a passionate woman, you just had to get past the first time. It'll be enjoyable the next time."

Dyna cleaned the blood with the water and leaves and cursed under her breath. "There won't be a next time."

Thunder was roaring over their heads now, so he helped her dress and then tugged her to their horses, glad to see her horse had stayed near his stallion. He tossed her up onto hers and mounted his own, intending to lead her back to a spot he'd passed. It had looked like a cave.

"I'm not going anywhere with you," she shouted over the thunder. "I'm going to that cave ahead and you need not join me."

"Aye, I saw that cave and 'tis large enough for

both of us. We're going together. I'll not have you sitting around getting drenched. The fever was bad enough last time."

She didn't argue, something he didn't like, but he cared more about seeing her to safety at the moment. So he led her horse back to the cave, left the animals under the shelter of some hardy trees, and lifted her down and carried her inside. He didn't wish to let her go so he sat on a rock and settled her on his lap.

Neither said anything for a few minutes, just leaning against each other. Then Dyna mumbled, "That wasn't so great. I thought it was supposed to be wonderful." She settled her head against his shoulder.

"It will be next time, Diamond." He rubbed her back lightly. Hellfire but he'd done everything wrong. He should have known to handle things differently.

Because Dyna was so gloriously different from most lasses.

"There'll be no next time." The set in her jaw-line told him she wasn't making a jest. She meant what she said, even though he felt certain she'd change her mind.

"Hmmm. You're too passionate to stay celibate forever. You'll want to finish."

"There was naught to finish. You liked it and you finished, but I didn't." Her pursed lips took on the look of a pouting bairn. She apparently was as sexually frustrated as he was, but he'd not let her know. And she also didn't understand the act well enough to interpret what had transpired.

"I didn't finish, Diamond." He lifted her chin so she stared into his eyes. "'Twasn't nice for me either. I hated hurting you, and 'tis rather frustrating to start and not finish."

"Well, I don't know what that means, but I better not be carrying a bairn. How will I know?"

The bluster had all gone out of her, and he hated it. He had to do something to give her back her fire. Hellfire, he'd gone mushy over her and it didn't even bother him. "Lass, you can't be carrying a bairn if I never gave you my seed."

"But you put it in me. How would you know if you gave me your seed? You must have. It hurt enough."

"Diamond, when I give you my seed, you'll know it. Finishing will be pleasurable, for both of us, even if we don't finish together. But I'll know when you do, and you'll know when I do. 'Tis part of what makes it special."

"What? I don't understand."

She looked up at him with a look of innocence he rarely saw in her, and it caught him again that perhaps she did have a softness inside that he'd never noticed.

He had to try to explain it to her. "Making love is about giving pleasure to someone you care for. 'Tis supposed to be a special moment between two people. It should be two people who love each other." He lifted his brows. "Mayhap 'tis why we failed. We don't love each other enough."

"So that's it. You don't love me." She pushed

against his chest.

"Mayhap you don't love me either." He had to say something to enrage her a bit so the old Dyna would emerge. Then it came to him. This was sure to get the fire going again. "You said you adored me, but you obviously don't."

The flash in her eyes was nearly instantaneous, and he fought to hide his grin.

"I never said any such thing. I *don't* adore you. Where did you dream that up?"

He let himself smile, grateful to see that fierce look in her eyes again. Grateful he had his Dyna back. "Listen. We don't need to overthink this. I'm sorry I hurt you, but the next time we do it, we'll both finish and then you'll understand." He rubbed her arms to warm her. "No rain, no thunderstorms, no interference."

"There won't be any next time."

"Like bloody hell there won't be. You'll want me again, and I'll want you again, and it will happen, but next time 'twill be pleasurable for both of us. Now stop thinking on it. What the hell are you doing traveling alone? Why did you leave without any guards?" He glanced up at the dark sky, the rain slowing a bit as the clouds rolled and twisted and turned unlike anything he'd ever seen. "You shouldn't be in a storm like this alone. Your horse could toss you from the shaking of the ground. I've never seen the like."

Then her whole countenance changed. "They mustn't have told you. Grandsire is missing. He only stayed at Cameron land one night before leaving. No one knows where he went, but something happened to him. I can feel it. So I rode out to find him."

"Alone? What the hell are you thinking?"

"I'll admit you are correct. I shouldn't have left on my own, but I had one of my dreams. I heard Grandsire say he was going to turn himself over to the English." She fussed with her hair. "I wasn't thinking clearly. I'm cold."

He moved her off his lap and said, "I'll go find some wood and start a fire. You wait here." He surveyed the area, looking for the driest spot, then found what might be the last remaining dry log in the forest, which he cut up and carried back to the cave, starting a fire quickly.

They watched the rain, and he listened to Dyna talk about her father, her grandsire, and her sister.

"Tell me the truth, Diamond. Do you truly believe he gave himself over to the English?" He knew the man to be wily, a crafty old goat who kept everyone guessing, but he was also a warrior. He couldn't picture the great Alexander Grant handing himself over to the enemy, especially the King of England. They all had despised King Edward, father and son. "He'd not willingly leave you and your family. Even John and Ailith. He adores them. My guess is 'twas just a nightmare, not one of your seer's dreams."

She yawned. "I *am* overtired. It seemed so real, but it doesn't make sense to me either. My grandsire is not a quitter."

He kissed her forehead. "I agree. Glad to see your

mind is showing the keenness I know so well. We'll have to go back and see what your father found out on Cameron land. Now the other. Claray says someone is watching her?"

"She said someone watches from the wall."

"How did she describe the person? A man?"

"She never actually saw the person." She paused. "You don't understand my sister. She gets upset when the people in her life aren't around. With Grandsire gone, with me gone, she was bound to start having some odd dreams. I have to prove all of her fears unfounded. Sometimes she thinks there's a giant spider having babies outside her window or that the creatures are hiding in the shadows, waiting for dark to attack our mother. She's had many such worries over the years."

"Poor thing." He couldn't imagine being so tormented as a child. He may have lost his parents at a young age, but he'd been close enough to manhood. Things could have been much worse for him and Joya.

"I try to help out where I can. Mama and Papa have done much, too, yet it continues."

"Do you think 'tis possible Claray is really being watched? And if so, who could possibly be watching her?" He pulled her closer and sat with her tucked in front of him, giving her the warmth of the fire. The way she fit into him, as if his body had been left with a hollow meant just for her, erased any doubts he'd still harbored about their future. He may not be worthy of her, but he would do whatever she asked of him, even if he wasn't ready to admit that to her yet.

"I still suspect she's imagining it. The footprints could have belonged to anyone. I don't know what to do to help her, but once she gets a fear in her head, it doesn't leave her."

"Where were you headed? I know you were looking for your grandsire, but what was your final destination?"

She sighed deeply, and he snuck a look at her. "I don't know," she said, with what sounded like a catch in her voice. "I left without thinking. I thought to look for any evidence of a struggle, but that waking dream about my grandfather sent me off in a hurry. Following the main path probably wasn't the smartest plan, but 'tis strange that I've searched all day without finding any evidence of a skirmish or any dead horses or guards. Of course, if there'd been anything like that, my sire would likely have seen it first, but again, I wasn't thinking."

"So you were heading toward Cameron land?"

"Aye and nay," she answered sheepishly. "I was heading toward Grandsire. Sometimes after I have a dream like that, I allow the heavens or the winds or whatever lead me." She met his gaze without flinching or backing down. "I'm usually able to find my way to the spot the angels, or whomever, wish me to find, but nothing materialized this time. Still, I can't just sit around and wait, Derric. I need to do something." The way she constantly kneaded her hands told him exactly how much she meant it.

"How about this? How about if we spend the night here and head back to Grant land at first light. We'll see if anyone has returned or if there have been any other messengers. Mayhap your grandsire is home safe, and if not, I would at least like to ask for a few Grant guards or Alick and Branwen to travel with us. Or we could wait for the rest of the Highland Swords. Mayhap you and your cousins are meant to find him together."

She bent her knees and set her chin on her knees. "Aye, I know you're right. A part of me knew it was a mistake even as I was doing it."

"And you'll promise to stay here with me this eve and not leave until first light?"

"Aye. We'll go back on the morrow. We aren't that far away, and Papa could have returned. While I slept a wee bit at home, I am still overtired."

He enveloped her in his arms again to give her his heat. "Where else could your grandsire have gone? He is a grown man, the past leader of one of the greatest clans in all the Highlands. He only does things after careful thought is my guess."

"Many places. Too many to consider. And before I agree to sleep here with you, you must promise not to touch me like that again. I'm sore."

"I promise, as long as you'll allow me to hold you. You can put your back against my chest. Will that suit you?"

"Aye."

She sighed so deeply that he knew how much she hurt inside, far more than the pain between her legs.

Why did that make him feel worse?

A sudden stab of irony hit him. He was witnessing another side of that soft heart her grandfather had told him about. She was so overprotective of the people she loved that she put herself at risk.

Her diamond shell was quickly becoming a pearl.

He may have just completed his quest.

Dyna awakened in the middle of the night, not surprised to feel overheated from the massive man plastered across her. Slipping out from under his arms, she managed to find her way out of the cave in the dark to take care of her needs without awakening him.

The nights in the Highlands were her favorite. She loved sitting beneath the stars, listening to the night sounds, her favorite being the hoot of an owl. So she lowered herself in front of the entrance to the cave, hugging her body against the night, and listened. As if answering her call, an owl cried out.

There was enough of a breeze to stir the leaves on the ground. Glancing over her head, she thought of the night she and Derric had stargazed together. If only she could go back to that simpler time, when her grandfather and Claray had both been safe.

Before she had lost her maidenhead.

She'd have to apologize to Derric when he awakened. She'd not been fair to him, but the entire situation had taken her by surprise. Normally, she had a strong tolerance for pain, but this pain had come in the midst of unimaginable pleasure. It had caught her by surprise, like a betrayal.

And her instinct had been to push back at the pain. At him.

She jumped when Derric touched her shoulder, alerting her to his presence, and then wrapped his arms around her from behind once he sat down. Settling his chin on her shoulder, he whispered, "I'm sorry, Diamond. If I could have done it without hurting you, I would have."

"Derric, you need not apologize. I acted like a wee bairn, and I don't know why." She leaned back against him. "I knew it was supposed to hurt. It wasn't even that bad, it just surprised me. I never asked you what you found out about Senga."

"I met wee Senga," he said with a chuckle. "Her father, to whom she bears an uncanny resemblance, named her after her mother. She is well cared for and happy, which is what I wished to learn."

"Did you have any regrets when you found out she wasn't yours?" She turned around to face him, wanting to see his expression.

"A wee bit. That surprised me, although I knew it was for the best. Her father is quite taken with her, has a mother at home to help him, so I left without admitting why I was there. No need to say anything."

She reached up and straightened some of his hair, wild from sleep. "You're a wise man, Corbett."

He arched a brow at her, a doubtful look.

"And I'm starting to really like having you around." She leaned forward and kissed him. "I hope you'll stay with me. I'm sorry I keep trying to push you away. It's...it's not what I want."

He paused before he spoke, and she wondered what thoughts carried through his mind. How she hoped he'd accept her, quirks and all. She was a unique individual and her parents had never tried to change her. For that, she would be eternally grateful, but she didn't know if any man could accept her odd ways.

He said, "Every time I'm near you, all I want to do is move closer. You have an odd pull on me. I'm enjoying our time together."

"Even when we bicker?"

"Especially when we bicker. You challenge me, Dyna, and somehow I think I'll be a better man because of it. Until this chaos gets straightened out, you can expect to see me whenever you turn around."

She scowled but was still pleased by this declaration.

"Somebody has to watch over you, lass. You're too careless and arrogant by far."

"Arrogant? I think you're speaking of yourself, Corbett. That swagger, that grin."

He squeezed her shoulder, then stood and made his way toward the trees. As he strode away, she called out, "That arse."

"Just keep watching it. I know you can't help yourself."

CHAPTER NINETEEN

SHE SLEPT WAY PAST DAWN, and when she awoke, she searched for the heat that had surrounded her the night before. "Derric?" she said, panicked for a moment. Had he left after all?

But he entered the cave as soon as she called his name, carrying a skin of water that he held out to her. The first thing he asked was, "Are you hale?"

"I'm fine. But we must move quickly." She didn't let on how much she'd enjoyed sleeping in his arms last night, but someday she promised herself she would. He was kind, protective, and funny, and a fierce warrior besides. Kissing him left her breathless.

What more could she want?

They arrived back at the castle shortly after high sun. She was surprised to see so many guards surrounding the castle, though none stopped them. In fact, they nearly made it to the gates before her father spied her and charged directly toward her.

"Where the hell have you been, Dyna?"

"I went searching for Grandsire. You were gone,

and I couldn't sit still," she replied, not backing down. She'd pay for this transgression eventually, but probably not until her father found Alex Grant. All of the Highlands would be searching for him soon.

"You've gone off on your own before, but you're usually wise enough to travel with guards. What the hell were you thinking? And where did you find Derric?"

"I wasn't thinking. I went out to look for evidence of Claray's stalker, thinking I'd stay on our land, but then I had this vision about Grandsire so I just kept riding. Derric came looking for me after he found out I wasn't at Clan Grant. He agreed to help."

He nodded tersely. "Did you see anything?" he asked, indicating for the two of them to follow him to the stables.

"Nay. What did Uncle Aedan say?" she asked. "He was with Grandsire when last I saw him."

They'd reached the stables, and Connor dismounted. He reached up to help Dyna down, and she gripped his shoulders a little too hard. She regretted it as soon as she did it—what if he guessed?—but she couldn't have stopped herself if she'd tried.

She was still sore and riding a horse hadn't helped.

"What's wrong with you?" her father asked, his eyes narrowing as he set her down on the ground.

"Naught. Tell me what you learned, Papa. You know you're tormenting me by making me wait." Mayhap she should be a wee bit sweeter, considering she'd run off by herself to search for Grandsire, but she had to draw his attention away from her pain.

"Aedan said he left on his own accord. He said he had somewhere to go and he would return. They didn't expect him to be gone for long, but he hasn't come back."

"And he didn't say where he was headed?"

"Nay, which is not unlike my father. He doesn't always see fit to share his plans with everyone, especially in his younger days, but it surely unsettles me."

"Did the guards go with him?"

"Aye, six of them according to Aedan." Her father looked over her head at another group approaching them. "Well, word travels quickly. Your cousins are here. We'll see what they've heard."

Dyna spun around, pleased to see Alasdair, Emmalin, Els, and Joya dismounting near the stables with a dozen guards. Alasdair was giving instructions to his men, but Dyna didn't care. She had to find out if they'd heard of anything at all.

"Well? Have you heard about Grandsire? Seen him anywhere?" she shouted to them, too impatient to wait.

"Naught. We've heard naught. When are you heading out again?" Alasdair asked. "We must find him."

Her father waved them forward. "My thanks for coming so quickly. We'll meet inside and discuss our strategy. I want input from Jamie and Finlay. You all need to rest. We'll make a plan and probably divide into groups. Head out in an hour or two."

Dyna greeted her cousins quickly, then leaned over to speak to Derric, trying to be discreet, "I'm headed to the bathing chamber, then I'll join you in an hour. I'd like to hear what Papa comes up with." He nodded and made his way over to Joya.

Recognizing her opportunity to escape—her sire was still speaking with Alasdair—Dyna whirled around and raced up the steps to the keep, ignoring the slight pain between her legs.

She had the sudden realization that she was different, and no one but Derric knew.

Claray greeted her and followed her up the stairs to her chamber. "Did you find my stalker?"

"Nay. I'm sorry. I did find evidence that someone was behind the curtain wall, but I couldn't find him. The footprints could have been caused by anyone. Claray, just stay inside, don't go anywhere alone, and we'll find him, if he is there, after we locate Grandsire."

The tears came quicker that she'd expected. "You don't believe me either. Everyone treats me like I'm daft, but he was there, Dyna. I tell you, he was there."

"Did you see him last eve?" she asked, pulling her hair out of its plait so she could wash it. She grabbed a clean tunic and leggings and headed to the bathing chamber, Claray following her.

"Nay, he wasn't here last eve. There have been too many people around."

"Good, then mayhap he'll leave you be," she said,

opening the door to the chamber. "Do you wish to bathe, too?"

"Nay," Claray mumbled, the dejection on her face telling Dyna all she needed to know.

"I have to wash up, and then we'll go out after Grandsire." She leaned over and hugged Claray. "I promise to help, but first we have to find Grandsire."

Claray nodded and left, and Dyna was left with the sinking feeling that she'd failed her sister, too.

Derric led the group through the woods. He was pleased he had something to contribute to the effort to find Alex. The lairds believed it possible that Alex might have met with King Robert, offered to help him in his final push to win the Highlands. And so they were riding back to the king's camp.

The Highland Swords group had agreed to travel together, while Connor, Jamie, and Finlay had ridden back toward Cameron land to see if Aedan had learned anything new. Since they had no idea where Alex had gone, or why, they needed to explore different possibilities.

Both groups traveled with plenty of guards, which pleased Derric because Joya and Branwen and Emmalin had all come along. He hadn't expected Emmalin to leave her bairns.

Then again, she was a true believer in the spectral swords. "Together, we can find him and save him," she'd said. "I believe it with all my heart, but someone must get us closer to him."

Joya drew her horse abreast of his. There was enough noise and conversation among the group that he knew they could speak freely without fear of being overheard. But had he known what she wished to talk about, he would have galloped ahead.

"Brother dear, what happened between you and Dyna? You did it, didn't you?"

His head whipped around so quickly he'd probably have a sore neck later. "What?"

"Don't play innocent with me. She's different. You did what she wanted and she's changed her mind about it."

Dumbfounded that she had guessed so accurately, he glanced behind him at Dyna, two horses back. She stared off into the horizon, her face filled with sadness. "You do know she's verra upset her grandsire is missing."

"Aye, but you didn't answer my question, did you?" His sister had a small smirk on her face that told him she knew the truth anyway.

"Nay, I did not dodge you. Some things are private, do you not agree?"

Joya turned her head to assess him carefully. "I suppose they should be, I grant you that. Dyna is a fine lass, but I doubt that she has much experience with other men. You are far more worldly than she is."

"And your reason for telling me this?"

"I want you to guard her heart. She is not used to talking about her feelings the way most lasses are, which is not to say she doesn't have them. Please treat her well and be kind about everything."

"I'm trying my best, but sometimes I'm a fool, I guess." He didn't know how else to explain his inability to make things right with Dyna.

"Dyna has many other things demanding her attention right now—her grandsire, her sister, even her mother. Don't be too hard on her. Once this all settles, you'll be able to work things out. I think she's good for you, brother. And you for her."

Derric couldn't argue with her reasoning. "Tell me what you know about the spectral swords. Emmalin insisted the three of you needed to come along. Why?"

"'Tis hard to explain, but Alex Grant believes the spouses are part of the magic, if that's what you wish to call it. You've witnessed the power before. Don't you believe in our strength together?"

"I can hardly deny it given I was in the middle of it, with Dyna crawling up my back. I saw the thunderstorm, felt the ground shake, watched the enemies drop quicker than in any other battle. Where does the storm come in? Is that where the power originates?" He had a faint memory of the start of a thunderstorm last night, yet it hadn't continued for long.

"I don't think any of us completely understand how it works. Dyna is the one who unleashes the power somehow, by raising her weapon over her head, and it channels into the others' swords."

"But do you believe in it?" he asked, his gaze locked on hers as he awaited her answer.

"Aye, I do. There is something special about the cousins. Wee John too. His presence has an effect on the unnatural storms the power brings. I've witnessed it more than once so I have to be a believer. Aren't you?"

He couldn't deny what he'd seen. "I am. I hope it proves its value again in this search for Alex, but we don't have John."

"Indeed, we do not. We can only hope we'll be enough. Now, I wonder why Dyna is keeping her distance from you?" She clucked her tongue. "I hope 'tis just because she's upset about her grandsire and naught else."

He gave her a look, and she laughed. "I'm going to join Els. Godspeed and be careful with her, Derric."

He nodded as she moved ahead of him to join her husband, finding a space on one side of him.

Little did Joya know she'd struck a sore point. Derric had hoped Dyna would ride beside him. That she would speak to him. But although he'd gotten half of his wish—she *was* riding near him—she hadn't said a word. She was distraught and tired, if he were to guess. And yet a part of him was disappointed that she'd turned away from him in her distress rather than toward him.

Alasdair pulled his horse abreast of Dyna's. "Anything at all? You must use your seer abilities to find him. Think, Dyna."

"I am," she snapped. "Do you not think I was doing that yestereve when I searched for him?"

"How much farther to Robert's camp, Derric?"

Els shouted. "Can we get there within the hour? If not, we should find our own place to camp this eve."

"Half the hour."

"Lead on, then. I wish to know this eve if Grandsire is there," Dyna said.

"And I'll thank you for granting me the pleasure of speaking to me, Diamond. I was starting to think you'd prefer to curse me." He glanced over his shoulder, catching enough of a glimpse of her to see her glare. It put a smirk on his face. At least she wasn't down. He'd rather see her mad than downtrodden.

"Corbett, I can lead the way if you're lost." Bloody hell, but the woman was as sexually frustrated as he was, for certes. You couldn't participate in that kind of passionate foreplay and just forget it had happened. She'd be tough to win over, but he would, and he'd have her screaming with pleasure if it was the last thing he did.

First, they had to find Alexander Grant.

They were close enough to the camp to be heard by the guards so he let out a bird call, letting Robert's warriors know he was a friend. When he received an answer, he led the group into the king's camp.

They dismounted and tied their horses, moving toward the large tent in the middle. He expected King Robert to greet them. His usual approach was to greet all new entrants to the camp, but this time he didn't.

The king sat on a large boulder and held his hand

up to the group. "You only, Corbett." Many of his men had to be on patrol because the area looked almost deserted. The king only had four guards nearby, and from the look of them, their specific duty was to protect him.

The situation took him by surprise, but he turned to the others and said in an undertone, "I'll find out what has transpired. 'Tis most unlike him not to greet us personally." He hoped it wasn't because of what he feared. The only other time he'd seen their king turn people away was when he was ill. A leader never wanted his enemy to know he was sickly.

"Make sure you ask about Grandsire," Dyna prodded.

"Of course, I will, Diamond. I'm as anxious to find the man as you are."

She gave one of her unladylike snorts and tossed her opinion at him. "I doubt that."

He knew it wouldn't do any good to argue with her, not in the mood she was in, and truthfully he was concerned about the change he saw in King Robert, so he left the cousins and turned toward the king's rock.

"King Robert, you are hale?" he said as he approached, bowing a bit. The king, usually so quick to greet others, stayed seated. His color was pale and his eyes tired. Something was not right.

"In secret, I'll admit I feel a bit unwell, but I won't allow it to stop me. Fortunately, I've no need to go to battle soon."

"Have you postponed it?" Days ago, the king had

seemed intent on using might to win what diplomacy could not: the allegiance of the Scots who still sided with the English.

"To my surprise, we've been able to form a truce of sorts with both Ross and Thane. They sent a messenger, and we shall meet later to finalize the terms. Ross does not wish for a battle. And even though I'd love nothing better than to show the man what loyalty looks like—and how disloyalty is justly repaid—I'm grateful that I don't have to do it just yet. I'll agree to this truce for a year, but we will revisit this again. I have unforeseen circumstances forcing my hand."

Derric had to admit, the king did look unwell.

He let out a deep sigh, taking his time to gather his breath. "As you can see, I'm not well enough to go to battle. The old intestinal ailment has plagued me since last eve. You've found the Grant lass, I see."

"Aye, and her cousins are with me."

"The mighty Alexander Grant left this morn. The English didn't get to him, after all. He's an amazing man."

"He was here?" Derric tried not to shout, though it was beyond frustrating to know Alex had been and gone. If he'd stayed instead of going after Dyna, he would have found him. "Where was he going? Who was with him? We've been looking for the man for days."

"He was not suffering and came of his own free will," Robert said. "I wasn't about to issue orders to him. He said he was heading south again. Came to see if he could be of assistance. Spoke with some others in the camp, then took his leave."

Hell, he'd have to make sure they were far away from the king before Dyna learned of this information.

The next instant, Dyna came up to stand beside Derric. Although the king had asked for a private audience, Derric wasn't surprised by her boldness—if anything, he'd thought she would join him sooner. "King Robert, did I hear you say my grandsire was here?" She did well to hide her emotions because he guessed she was quaking inside. "Was he hale?"

"Stronger than I am, apparently. He slept on the ground last eve, spoke to several people in the camp, then left this morn. You are worried, I see."

"He hasn't spoken with any of us. We feared the worst."

"The man is a great leader of many Scots. You don't trust him to use good judgment?"

Dyna shuffled her feet and stared at the dirt. "He *is* a great leader, but he told us he was headed to Cameron land and left the next day without sharing his destination. We thought something had happened to him. With King Edward and his threats…"

"Lass, Cameron land is not far. And Grant land is south of here. Perhaps he's headed home. And as for Edward, the yellow-bellied beast, your grandsire is far enough in the Highlands that he needn't worry about a direct attack. Edward's son does not have the constitution his sire had. You'll never see him out in this cold. He's back in his royal castle with his friends, servants doting on his every need. I wouldn't worry about it. I think Alexander Grant can take care of himself."

"Did he still have guards with him?"

"Aye, six or eight is my guess. You're welcome to spend the night here. This land can be treacherous in the dark, as you know. You can find him in the morn."

The king's eyes fluttered shut but jerked back up again. Derric set his hand against the small of Dyna's back and did his best to turn her away from Robert. "Our thanks for your help. Get your rest, King Robert. I'm sure you'll be feeling better by morn."

King Robert nodded, stood up slowly, and made his way back toward his tent. He paused at the entrance and said, "Godspeed to you. I pray I'm right and no one is after your grandfather. 'Tis time for our people to be the power they were intended to be."

They returned to the rest of the group and explained what they'd heard, giving them a moment to gather their thoughts.

Alasdair was the first to respond. "At least Grandsire's not a prisoner of the English. Perhaps the king is right. He could be headed to Grant land. Mayhap he visited Uncle Brodie at Muir Castle along the way. That would fit. I think we can take our rest and follow on the morrow. Everyone agree?"

"Aye," Els said. "I still don't like that he's off on his own without any of us, but for all we know he simply left Cameron land because he thought it best to stay on the move. To keep the English guessing. He has guards with him and could be headed home now."

Alick nodded. "It sounds as if he came to help Robert, then left when he found out he wasn't needed. And he had Grant guards with him, aye?"

"Aye," Derric replied. "He said six or eight."

Emmalin said, "I'm exhausted. Can we not sleep for a wee bit before moving on?"

"Aye," Joya agreed. "I'll not get back on that horse again right now for anything."

Since Branwen was also in agreement, they found a spot under a copse of trees. Alasdair had brought a tent for cover because his wife was along, and Els had a tarp for the others to sleep on to help them stay dry. They clustered together, the three married couples cuddling close. As usual, the guards had found a spot on the periphery for their own camp, and three of them stood guard. The watch would shift in a few hours.

That left Dyna and Derric. She'd already made it clear she didn't want to get too close to him, but surely she wouldn't deny herself the benefit of his heat.

Derric came up behind her and whispered, "We're in a crowd of your cousins. I'll be on my best behavior, but you know you could use my warmth. You said you liked it last eve." He knew she was not one to make any declarations in front of anyone, but he didn't understand why she would turn him away. It wasn't as if he'd make a display of them or run about telling her cousins what had taken place last eve. He liked his bollocks just fine where they were. "I'll say naught, just settle."

She sighed and stared up at him, pondering her choices.

Although he'd spoken for only her ears, her hesitation must have been obvious to the others—along with the reason for it—because Alick said, "Don't be a fool. You're fully clothed in the middle of your cousins."

"Aye," Joya said, "and his sister would kick his arse if he touched you inappropriately."

Dyna glanced at Joya, finally agreed, and lay down close to him.

But she wouldn't let her skin touch his.

Close as they were, they might as well have been a mountainside apart. The ice she gave off was as frosty as ever. He thought they'd settled everything, so why was she denying him?

Could he have been mistaken about how she felt?

CHAPTER TWENTY

ALEXANDER GRANT WAS TIRED. TIRED of searching over half the Highlands for the person he sought. It wouldn't be long before someone from his clan found him and he'd be forced to go back to Grant land.

But he couldn't.

He was done watching his clan be tortured by the English.

The last plan he'd made had failed—the Scottish sheriffs hadn't been stationed near King Robert like he'd thought. His confidant had done as promised, but he couldn't keep asking for help.

It was time to complete this mission.

He awakened early that morn and stood on his favorite vantage point, looking down at the snow-topped Highland mountains he so loved. He only knew one person who liked this view more than he did.

His companion joined him. "'Tis a view I've always loved, but you know that. We've seen much happen in the Highlands over the years, and I still treasure every single trip I've made across this point."

Alex clasped the man's shoulder. "Aye, we've seen much. I'd hoped to see Scotland back in control of the Scots before I leave this land. I hope King Robert will be successful. This move I'm about to make should seal that for all of our countrymen."

The other man pointed. "Look below. The ones you're searching for are there, I believe."

Alex squinted, cursing his loss of vision. "I cannot see that far any longer. I must depend on your eyes."

"Trust me that the man you are looking for is ahead of us. 'Tis time for us to move."

Alexander Grant smiled and squared his shoulders. "Lead on. We'll end this."

Dyna awakened early and intentionally made enough noise to rouse Derric. He sat up and said, "You couldn't leave us be for another hour, Diamond?"

"Nay. We have to move on."

Derric rubbed his eyes and stared at her. "You're certain we must go now?"

"Aye, *I* must. You need not travel with me. You can follow with the others."

Els apparently overheard them, for he sat up and said, "Slow down and see if you can pick up on anything other than your bad feeling. Do you have any reason to think Grandsire is in trouble?" He pushed himself to standing, groaning as he straightened his back after sleeping on the ground.

"Busby. DeFry. I have this feeling they've found him. And someone else, but I can't wait. I had a dream." She closed her eyes and put her head in her hands, trying to remember the exact details. "Grandsire is going with them to see Edward's son." She opened her eyes and stared at the group. "Hurry. We have to stop them. 'Tis a trap."

Els studied her carefully. "Are you certain, Dyna?"

Dyna was already on her feet, hurrying toward her mount. She had to get to her grandfather and stop him. The clarity had come to her, and now she needed to move. To head toward him.

"You can follow me," she said to Els. "You and the others. You'll have to catch up."

Alasdair sat up abruptly. "What the hell is happening?" he said, his voice thick with sleep.

Els said, "Dyna had a dream that Grandsire is with Busby and DeFry and they're going to see King Edward."

"Then get up," he said, rising to his feet. "Alick, get your arse up," he said, giving him a little shove. "We're going after Grandsire. Dyna, wait for us."

"Nay, I'm not waiting. Follow me."

"You're not going alone if I have to tie you down," Alasdair growled. "We'll awaken the others and go together."

"I'll not be alone. Derric said he'd go with me. We'll wait for you at the overlook."

Els waved them on and leaned down to awaken Joya. Two minutes later, they were all awake and mumbling. But she was already mounted, ready to leave. She shot Derric an impatient look as he mounted his horse.

"Can you tell me exactly what happened in your dream?" he asked, a little breathless.

Dyna nodded, secretly glad he was coming. She didn't know how to explain the things she knew— or how she knew them. Sometimes it happened when awakened, and the knowledge was imparted in a dream. Sometimes it came to her from out of nowhere. Either way, she had learned not to ignore the waves of intuition. Even though she prayed she was wrong this time.

They headed out, following the path that would take them down out of the mountains toward Grant land. After they'd traveled far enough that they could ride abreast, she allowed him next to her. "I know what he's doing and why he's on his own."

"Why?" Derric asked out of the corner of his mouth. He'd already dipped into his saddlebag for an oatcake and shoved half of it in his mouth.

"He's giving himself to King Edward in return for the king's promise not to bother our clan any-more. It's the same as what I saw in my other vision. After hearing Edward still wants his head on a pike, he's decided to give him what he wants."

"Why the hell would he do something so fool-ish?" Derric bellowed out to the clouds above them.

"Because he doesn't want anyone else kidnapped because of him. Think on it. We nearly lost John and then Aunt Kyla. He planned this whole trip to get away from us."

They'd have to make their way down the mountain, but Dyna felt certain this was the same path Grandsire would take. He always stopped at his favorite place to look over the mountaintops.

It was the view he loved best other than the view from his own parapets.

Alex Grant caught up with the sheriffs. "Busby, I'll speak with you privately."

Busby stepped away from the others. DeFry was busy skinning rabbits with the few guards they had with them, and Alex's men stood back per his instructions.

"Grant," he murmured quietly, his beady eyes focused on him. "I'm surprised to see you traveling with so few guards. Not your usual way."

"You made a point to stop at my grandson's castle and warn him that English garrisons were out looking for me. Is this not true?"

"Aye, King Edward still wants your head on a pike, but he's not about to search for you himself in the cold. He's sending others for you."

"Know you any of the garrisons?" Alex asked, staring off into the distance.

"I do. Why?"

"I'm willing to deal with the Englishman in return for a promise."

Busby glanced over his shoulder, telling Alex that his guess was correct. Busby was not loyal to the Scottish. He was a traitor, unlike DeFry.

"What promise?" The words were spoken in an undertone, Busby clearly hoping not to reveal himself to DeFry.

"A promise to leave my clan be. I'll turn myself over if King Edward pledges to leave the rest of my clan alone."

The traitor couldn't hide his excitement over this revelation, and Alex wanted to reach over and choke him. But he kept quiet.

"I'll take you to the garrison, but without DeFry and without your warriors. Then you have my word your clan will be left alone." The purse of his lips told Alex exactly what he needed to know.

Busby was a lying traitor.

But his character didn't matter.

"When?" Alex asked.

"I'll take you now."

"If you hurt my clan, you know you'll pay dearly. Clan Grant has many allies. Do with me as you see fit, but my clan is to remain unharmed."

"Aye, I'll see to it if you go with me now." He glanced over his shoulder, still watching to see if DeFry was paying attention. "I have one man who will travel with us."

"Who?"

"Hamish. He stands in the rear of the group, brushing my horse."

Alex glanced over his shoulder, and a quick spark of recognition struck him. He knew Hamish from somewhere in his past, but he'd met too many warriors over the years to recall where he'd met this one. If the man knew him, it could actually work out for the best. He might agree to help Alex when he arrived on English soil.

"Agreed. Now or I'll change my mind."

Busby smiled, an evil grin that told Alex even more about the bastard, but he'd already made up his mind. "Agreed."

CHAPTER TWENTY-ONE

SINCE THEY HAD REACHED AN area where they could ride abreast, Derric rode beside Dyna, intent on talking to her. This situation was too personal for her, and it was interfering with her judgment. "Mayhap we should wait for your cousins," he said. "If you are correct, and I trust that you are, then we could use the assistance of the spectral swords. I'm not fool enough to deny what I've seen with my own eyes, and we both know the power helped us retrieve Emmalin and your aunt Kyla. We're all here."

"Nay, I'll not wait. They'll meet us at the overlook if they're ready. If not... We could lose him if we stay back for too long, and I refuse to fail Grandsire."

He thought he heard her voice crack. "Diamond, no matter what you say or do, no one would ever think you'd failed your grandsire. Why would you say such a thing? He never would. You're the most loyal person I've ever met."

"I'm not doing well, of late. Did you forget that

Grandsire disappeared after he got to Cameron land? 'Tis my fault."

"You take too much upon your shoulders, and you talk as if he's a wee bairn. Think you he would not have gotten away if you'd escorted him to the keep?"

"Mayhap I should have stayed with him. Promised to escort him to Grant land. Something. I'm sick with worry."

Derric couldn't believe she was taking this situation onto her shoulders. "Alex Grant is just as capable of getting away from his sister as he is escaping from his granddaughter. You're being too hard on yourself."

"Nay, I'm not hard enough on myself. Claray is terrified someone is watching her, yet I left her alone. I doubt anyone's there, but she believes it. She always believes it. She's a mess, and I don't know how to help her." She swiped at her eyes. And a feeling of helplessness unfurled in Derric. He wanted to help her shoulder her problems—the responsibilities that clearly weighed on her—but he had no idea how to tell her to help her sister.

"Don't you think that helping Claray is more your mother's job?"

"'Tis mine, too. And Papa's. But Claray isn't getting better. She's worse now than she's been in a verra long time. How do I convince her that no one is watching her?"

"I don't know, Diamond, but you take too much fault on your shoulders. You give everything to your clan and to the spectral swords. How much more could you give?"

Dyna slowed her horse.

He could see the mountain top through the fluttering tree leaves, the wind picking up as they rode. Was that what drew her?

They climbed the peak, winding higher and higher, and she stopped at an overlook point, a spot where you could peer across the landscape at a mountaintop, quite a view he had to admit. "This is the place. Grandsire's favorite view."

Dismounting, she slowly walked over to the edge, the groves of pines waving in the breeze, and looked down. He moved over to stand beside her, his arm coming up to settle on the small of her back, and to his surprise, she didn't push him away.

Her horse began to act skittish, though he didn't know why, so Derric moved over to attempt to calm the big stallion.

"Derric, he always acts like that when we stop here." She glanced over her shoulder at the animal, stepped back to quickly pat his withers, then moved back to the overlook point.

Derric reached in his pocket for one of the apples he'd taken from the stables, then stood next to the beast who was now pawing at the ground. "'Tis alright, big man. You worry about your mistress, but she'll not go over the side." He continued to speak calmly to the animal while Dyna searched the area beneath them.

Then she spun around to stare at him, crossing her arms in front of her. "You have a talent with horses?"

"Nay, I'm just extra kind to them. Your grandsire said if you treat them right, they'll be loyal. I'm just trying to calm an animal extremely loyal to his rider, though you are ignoring him." Then he rubbed the horse's neck and spoke directly to the animal. "I know how you feel. She ignores me, too."

She narrowed her gaze to glare at him, then whirled around, letting him know she was done with the conversation. Her horse nickered, nuzzling his hand for another treat.

Then her entire countenance changed. One hand flew up to cover her mouth as she pointed to a spot on a path far beneath them. Derric rushed to her side to see what had caught her attention. There, a good distance beneath them, stood a group of men on horseback in a circle. The men looked like miniatures, too far away to be clearly identified.

"'Tis him. Grandsire. Oh, Derric. I think he's tied to a horse. And I don't see but one Grant plaid. His." Then she whipped her head around to stare at her horse. "'Tis why he acted up. He's verra in tune with Grandsire. He could smell him."

"Dyna, 'tis a long distance for your horse to pick up the scent of your grandsire. I don't think 'tis possible."

"'Struth! We're going down there." She pointed to her stallion. "Do you not see? He's telling me 'tis Grandsire. He's been taken captive and we cannot wait."

"Are you sure? 'Tis a long way down. 'Tis too far

for us to see ropes."

"There's no way to know until we're directly behind him." She raced to her horse and mounted with a leap that made his mouth part. "You do as you please, Derric. But I cannot wait for my cousins. I'm following them now."

Derric sighed, moving and mounting in one fluid movement.

"Then I'm coming with you."

Alex had been tied to his horse, but it was no matter—he'd always had a talent for directing his mount with just his knees. Midnight was distressed because of his containment, but he knew the beast would follow his lead.

Busby had told DeFry that he was leading Alex to a specific pathway he wished to take, after which he'd return. Alex was annoyed to be portrayed as a daft old man who'd gotten lost, even more so because DeFry hadn't thought to question it. Before they left, Hamish following, Alex gave instructions to his guards, loyal men who already knew precisely what to do when he was taken captive.

He knew his grandbairns would be upset, but they would follow him. He hoped they would come together, as a group, because he suspected he'd need the spectral swords to get out of this. But he also knew his headstrong granddaughter would be beside herself with worry.

He wished he could tell her there was no need.

Alex wasn't ready to say goodbye to wee John and Ailith yet. He suspected there could be another couple of grandbairns coming along soon, but he didn't prod.

The three men didn't go far before they came upon a small English garrison. Busby left Alex with Hamish and rode ahead to speak with the man in charge of the group.

"You don't remember me, do you, my laird?" Hamish whispered when he brought his horse abreast of Midnight.

"You look familiar," Alex said. "Were you one of my guards many years ago?"

"Aye. I lived on Grant land for years, trained every day in the lists. Do not worry, my laird. I'll help you get through this safely."

His words were those of a faithful man, but Alex noted that Hamish would not make eye contact with him. Not a good sign. Memories trickled back to him. "Why did you leave Grant land? If my old memory serves me properly, you left without saying a word to anyone. Just disappeared."

"I received word that my mother was severely ill, so I left in a state of panic. My pardon for not having acted more appropriately. I was young and foolish."

But Hamish still wouldn't make eye contact. He hadn't even turned his head toward Alex.

Alex knew better than to trust a man who wouldn't look him in the eye. He tried to recall more about Hamish's time as a Grant warrior, but at the moment his mind came up empty.

Busby returned and said, "The garrison will escort you to Berwick Castle, where the king is presently in residence. Hamish and I will follow, see that you're treated well."

"Treated well, my arse," Alex scoffed. "You're a traitor, so don't try to pretend otherwise."

Busby grabbed the bindings around his wrists, his expression a dark glower. "You'll regret saying that. I'll have my chance with you."

It was then Hamish finally looked at Alex.

His wide grin showed the two missing front teeth, the kind a fist to the face usually caused. Experience had taught him that a man who lacked those teeth had typically lost them because he was untrustworthy, confirming the inkling he had about the bastard. But that inkling also told him there was more to Hamish's story.

What the hell was it?

Dyna had hoped the brief interlude at the overlook would give her cousins a chance to catch up with them, but they were nowhere in sight. Well, she couldn't wait.

Derric might be right—they were too far to see ropes—but she still knew her grandsire was tied to that horse. His posture was different, and after all the years he'd been on horseback, it was unlikely he would change the way he rode now.

"Do you know where you're going, Diamond?" Derric asked quietly, just loud enough to be heard.

"They aren't moving that quickly. If we keep

moving, we'll catch up with them."

They moved on, silence settling between them. Before they'd traveled an hour, Dyna called back to him over her shoulder. "I'm sorry for the way I acted."

"What are you talking about?"

She knew she'd treated him poorly. Both the other evening, after he'd taken her maidenhead— at her bidding—and on the ride the previous day. It had felt strange to be around him after what they'd shared, knowing none of her cousins understood how their relationship had changed. And she'd felt strangely vulnerable. Growing up, her response to feeling vulnerable had always been to hide her tears. To act tougher. Being the lass, she'd always felt the need to seem more aloof than her other cousins, as if nothing bothered her.

And so she'd pulled away from him even though she'd asked him not to pull away from her.

"You didn't do anything wrong the other evening. I was as willing as you were. And it was wrong of me to treat you poorly on this journey. I didn't know how to act around the others. I *do* care about you."

She glanced back again and saw he was arching a brow at her. Mayhap she shouldn't have told him that now, as they descended the mountain on a narrow part of the path that prevented them from riding side by side, but then again, it was easier to speak more openly when she didn't have to look him in the eye.

"Apology accepted. And I wish I hadn't hurt

you. If I could take it back, I would."

"My thanks," she said. She felt that way too, didn't she? So why couldn't she stop thinking about Derric touching her, his hand between her legs, his…

"Why do you always insist on being so tough? You never express emotion except for anger. When you have every right to cry, you swipe your tears away and lift your chin. What are you afraid of?"

Hellfire, but he'd cut right to the core of her. "I'm not afraid. I just…I was always with three lads. I've spent my entire life trying to fit in, trying to be like my father and my grandsire."

They'd passed the narrowest section of the path so he drew abreast of her again. "There's naught wrong with showing emotion. It does not make you weak. Mayhap you wouldn't be so tough on yourself if you'd let your emotions show once in a while."

She glanced over at him, surprised he'd paid so much attention to her. Surprised that he understood her at such a deep level. Had anyone ever bothered to look so closely? She glanced at the forest next to them, checking the area for reivers, but nothing stood out to her. Her gaze returned to the path in front of them. Perhaps she could catch a view of her grandsire and the bastards who held him captive.

It had to be that distraction that led her astray. Always alert to her surroundings, she was totally taken off guard when a horse came out of the woods. Before she could grab her bow, an arm snaked around her waist and lifted her onto another man's lap.

She fought and managed to land one punch to the jaw of her attacker, but what happened next was something she'd never forget.

"Dyna, stop, would you? You're going to ruin everything, so I had to get you off the main path quietly."

"He's wearing a Grant plaid, Diamond," Derric said loudly. "Stop fighting."

Shock overtook her, but she stopped swinging and did her best to sit up as the horse slowed. Whipping her head around, she looked straight into her captor's eyes.

"Loki?"

CHAPTER TWENTY-TWO

LOKI GRANT GRINNED, LEADING HER back off the main path and shouting over his shoulder, "Kenzie, get her horse." He rode to a hidden clearing that had been concealed behind a thick line of trees. A quick glance told her Derric was following directly behind them. "I'm sorry for surprising you, but you would have ruined our plan."

"What are you doing here?" she asked, jumping down from his horse as he soon as they slowed down. "We have to go after Grandsire." When he finally dismounted and stood in front of her, she shoved at him.

Loki just gave her a sly grin. "Uncle Alex came to me after he left Cameron land. He wanted to make sure the English wouldn't kidnap any more Grants just to get to him." He stood there with his hands on his hips, over two score of warriors behind him, all wearing Grant plaids.

They had help.

"He told you? Why did he not tell me?" Her

insides twisted and turned at the thought that her grandfather trusted Loki more than her.

Apparently, she did a poor job hiding her feelings because Loki took one look at her and said, "Mayhap he asked me because he wanted to come at the English with a different force. They'd know to watch the Clan Grant warriors on your land, but no one would suspect my involvement. The English are quite ignorant, as you know. The man had his reasons," Loki said, patting her shoulder. "He asked for my assistance, and after all he's done for me, I certainly couldn't turn him down." As a bairn, Loki had been adopted by Alex's brother, Brodie, and his wife, Celestina, after they found him living in a crate behind a tavern. Alex Grant had given him his own castle, Castle Curanta, where he and his wife, Bella, took in other orphans and abandoned children. They also had two bairns of their own, a lad and a lassie.

"What exactly did he ask you to do?" Derric asked, jumping down from his horse. Then, as if realizing he had yet to introduce himself, he nodded. "Derric Corbett, pleased to meet you. I'm relieved we'll have your assistance in getting Alex Grant away from the English."

"Aye, we'll take care of them soon enough. Alex asked me not to tell anyone from his clan what he was planning until it was too late to stop him. I know you're upset he didn't confide in you, but if he had told you, you would have needed to tell your sire, your laird, his siblings, his children, and so on. I didn't have to tell anyone, so I could do what he asked without upsetting his clan and all his allies. Don't take it too hard, Dyna. But I think I'm safe revealing the truth now." He glanced back over his shoulder. "Uncle Alex told me to take the garrison out and leave no survivors. He aims to send a message, and that's exactly what we'll do."

Dyna turned to the sea of warriors that had been gathering behind Loki. She recognized many of them, and the sight brought tears to her eyes. She didn't swipe her tears away this time, instead allowing them to roll freely down her cheeks. She smiled and said, "Derric, on the left is Kenzie, next to him is Gillie, then you'll see Thorn and Nari, who helped my mother and father escape some cruel bastards. And he"—she pointed to one of the four—"is married to my aunt Elizabeth."

"You're going to attack soon?" Derric asked.

"Aye, we will. Dyna, why are you the only Grant here? I hardly think your grandsire would approve. He was expecting to see the rest of your group."

"Alasdair and Emmalin, Els and Joya, and Alick and Branwen will be along soon. They've been trailing us down the mountain. They'll help for certes."

"Any archers besides you?"

"Aye, Branwen and Emmalin." Emmalin had worked hard to build her skills, Dyna helping to train her whenever she visited MacLintock land. Joya was best at distraction.

Loki let out a low whistle. "Alex has told me about the spectral swords. I hope we get to witness you at full strength. But wee John and Ailith are safe?"

"Aye, they are on MacLintock land. Tell us what to do."

Loki stepped out of the trees to glance down the path. "We'll follow shortly, but you archers can go ahead if you can find your place quietly. We'll take them out from behind so they'll know not what hit them. Alex said he'll make his way to the front so as not to be close to the fighting. He suspected he'd be bound at this point."

"Loki, I'm so glad to see you. We'll get him back for sure."

"Aye, we will. We'll start without your cousins and hope they join us."

"How many in the garrison?" Derric asked.

Loki spit on the ground in front of him. "This is a small group. There are around four score surly Englishmen by my count to our five and forty, but we can take them. Especially if your cousins join us."

"Lead on," Dyna said, mounting her horse.

Her intuition had brought her straight to Loki. The situation was finally tilting in their favor.

The time was nigh. Alex tugged on his bindings, hoping he could free himself once Loki's group attacked, but the ropes were stronger than he'd anticipated.

He'd given Loki instructions on where he should attack, if possible. Just as he'd thought, Busby had brought him to the group of English cavalry. The group numbered around eighty, but Loki had at least two score. Everyone knew one Highlander could take out two to three Englishmen, so the numbers were good. He had complete confidence in Loki's warriors.

He also suspected his granddaughter would come along soon with the spectral swords. They'd assist as necessary. Once this was done, word of the defeat would pass through all the Highlands and Lowlands. Everyone would know a small group of Highlanders had crushed a much larger force of English.

He hoped it would be enough to keep Edward's son away until next summer.

Once he was free, he'd have the task of convincing the lass that Derric was meant for her. That he belonged with the spectral swords and would also make a fine addition to Clan Grant. Of course, he'd have to ensure Corbett had completed his quest, but if he'd spent this much time with Dyna, he must have seen her soft heart.

Unfortunately, the lass could be a wee bit stubborn. Somehow, he'd have to convince her Derric was the one for her.

Derric couldn't believe they were about to attack the English given they had only about half as many warriors. His gaze followed Dyna as she and two other archers took off to find good perches. Loki had told them where and when they would make their attack, and the archers were getting in place so they could do the most damage from the air, leaving their horses for Loki's men to manage.

The English bastards clearly had no idea there was a force behind them. They seemed to be too wrapped up in themselves—and their perceived victory—to listen for marauders. Based on their gestures and their raucous laughter, Derric suspected they were also taunting Alexander Grant for having been caught, but they wouldn't have the last laugh.

Once the archers were in position—Dyna gave a bird call—Loki led the charge with the Grant war whoop, attacking from behind and both sides. Derric rode with them, his horse as close to Dyna's location as he could get it. Arrows sluiced over his head, catching the daft Englishmen completely by surprise, but he focused on his own task and headed straight at three English staring at the arrows overhead. He swung his sword in a side arc, catching the first one by surprise with a sword strike to his middle. Blood drenched his tunic quickly before he fell off his mount. He caught the next one in his arm, knocking his weapon to the ground, and then finished by plunging his sword into the belly of the third man, who wrenched away and lost his mount. That gave Derric the opportunity to swing back and hit the second man with the flat of his blade, sending him flying off his horse.

They fought for what seemed to be hours but was probably only minutes. Derric felt his strength leak away. Bloody hell, but he'd fought so much better than in his last battle—all his sword practicing paying off for him—but he'd used up much of his strength. He'd never had to battle this many for this long before.

That's when he noticed what he'd dreaded. There were more English left than he would have expected at this point, especially given how hard they'd been hitting them. The English must have taken reinforcements because they appeared to come out of the trees, an endless supply of fresh men.

Another ten minutes didn't improve their standing, the Grant contingent now in the center of the path with English coming at them from three directions, the front and both sides. The attackers had become the targets. Derric took a small wound to his left arm that stunned him for a moment, but a shout from a nearby tree brought the battle back into focus.

"I'm fine, Diamond. Keep shooting."

Ten more minutes brought the force he'd been hoping for from the rear. Three powerful Grant war whoops announced the arrival of Alasdair, Els, and Alick, who charged into the battle with shocking intensity.

More arrows found their targets as Emmalin, and Branwen found their way into the trees, taking out ten men in a matter of moments because so many were shocked at the new addition to the Grant contingency.

They were still outnumbered by a large amount, and Derric feared for their lives. He'd never seen so many Englishmen in one place. Sweat dotted his brow even in the cool weather.

Dyna jumped down from her perch, and moments later, she rode out toward the melee, her bow lifted to the sky. When she joined Derric, she lifted her free hand across to him and he gripped it, holding on tight as if their connection meant life or death. Because to him it did. He loved this woman with all his heart and he wasn't about to lose her now.

The spectral swords had to work.

That's when it happened. With her bow aimed at the clouds, Dyna stared above their heads as the cloud formation began to swirl in a ferocious pattern, the winds coming up to toss the branches and leaves. Lightning forked through the air, the thunder not a moment behind it. The next strike sent two Englishmen flying through the air, one man snapping his neck when he landed.

The intensity of the storm ended the battle in a short time. He and Dyna lost their grip, but he could still feel the intensity of the storm and of *her* shooting through him. She was extraordinary. And together they would be something remarkable. The English were so distracted by the storm that the Grant cousins, who were fighting with an unnatural power and fury, were able to take out two to three men with one swing. They dropped faster than Derric had ever seen.

Once they were certain the skirmish had ended, Dyna glanced over at him and then rode hard, looking for her grandsire, he was sure. Loki joined her, and when Alasdair followed, Derric fell in behind him. He hadn't noticed Alex Grant at all during the battle, but Loki had said he would keep himself at the front, if at all possible.

But they reached the front without seeing any sign of him. They all stopped, except for Dyna, who continued to ride in circles, yelling, "Grandsire. 'Tis safe to come out now."

Derric glanced from one face to the next, and Loki said what they were all thinking. "Dyna, he's gone."

Alasdair rode forward and pointed to the ground. "He was taken captive by two men." The hoofprints of three animals were still fresh on the ground.

Derric cursed as Dyna joined them.

"He's with Busby and one other," she said.

But who was the other man and where had they gone?

Alex groaned and lifted his head, but the pain was too much for him. He was on a pallet in a small hut, and he thought he was alone. He recalled the battle, the lightning, but then something unanticipated had happened, putting a hitch in his plan.

Someone had struck him in the back of his head. Everything had turned black until now.

The pain in his head was so severe that he shut his eyes again, drifting into a dream that brought him pleasure.

Maddie stood in the loch, her back to him, dressed only in her chemise. Trembling from the temperature of the water, she glanced over her shoulder at him, her golden hair falling around her shoulders, the blue of her eyes visible from the distance.

"Alex, could you help me, please? The fabric is stuck in my wound."

He'd brought her to the loch to wash off her wounds, the ones her own brother had inflicted on her. Although they'd had many sweeter moments, this one was etched into his mind as one of the most important moments of his life because it was then he'd made his mind up. It was then he'd decided Madeline would be his wife. He remembered wondering if she'd give him a son or perhaps lassies.

"Alex?"

"Aye, I'd be pleased to help you, but you may wish to turn around. I must remove my plaid as 'tis the only one I have." He'd said it to guard her tender sensibilities, her innocence, as he waded into the water behind her. But when he took the soap from her hand, preparing to wash her, she said his name again.

"Alex?"

"Aye, Maddie?"

"You must push yourself to remember other things," she said, her tone turning urgent. "There is something you must recall. I know 'tis there in your mind, and you must pull it out. Things are not as they seem."

"Maddie? You're confusing me. I'm here to help you wash your back."

"Alex, 'tis a memory of our time together that you chose to revisit so I could come to you. Please don't forget that I can only be here for a short time. 'Tis verra difficult for me to appear to you."

"Why did you come this time?" he whispered, turning her around so he could gaze into her glorious blue eyes. "Can I not join you? I think I'm ready. 'Tis my time, nay?"

"Nay, Alex," she said, her tone intent. "Not yet. Don't you see? The spectral swords aren't only intended to project John—they need you. You are the one who'll guide your bairns and grandbairns through this terrible time in Scotland. Your clan and your country need you. Not yet, but do not worry. When your time comes, I'll be here waiting for you. Just a few more years."

"Maddie, I'm tiring…"

Her fingers came up to his lips to silence him. "It's not as you think. Busby is not out to get you. Hamish is."

"Hamish? But why?"

"Hamish wanted me, and I rejected him. Now he wants revenge. He'll try to get it through Dyna. Go!"

Maddie kissed him and walked off into the distance, giving him a small wave as she disappeared.

"You have to save Dyna," she said, her words pounding through his head.

He opened his eyes, driven by Maddie's last sentence, savoring her presence but forcing himself to search his surroundings.

He watched as Hamish and Busby entered the hut, Hamish behind the sheriff.

Hamish carried a large boulder. He lifted it and

brought it down upon Busby's skull.
Killing him instantly.

CHAPTER TWENTY-THREE

DYNA WAS FRANTIC. THEY'D MET as a group and agreed to split up, Loki taking his men toward his land to search for Alex while Dyna and her cousins headed toward Grant land. Those were the two major paths this far in the Highlands.

Busby and Grandpapa had to be on one path or the other.

Unless they'd taken him down some little used side path, although no one wanted to address that possibility.

"We're stopping on Grant land, Dyna," Els said. "I know you don't want to, but mayhap your sire or mine discovered something after we left. We could use a good meal before we move on to the next battle."

"There's also a chance Busby took him back toward Grant land, hoping to extort the use of our guards. They've tried it before. We don't know his intent. We will spend one night there, then move on." Alasdair cast a pointed look her way. Did everyone know what her plans would be? She had to admit, Alasdair knew her better than anyone.

Dyna clucked her tongue to keep from saying something she'd regret. "They won't be there—I know it—but aye, we should stop and change clothes. See if our sires are back. They need to send out more patrols. Loki's group and ours is not enough. You all know how difficult it is to track someone in the Highlands."

The others might not be ready to move along as quickly as she would want to. But Derric would go with her.

Wouldn't he?

Did she want him to go with her?

Hellfire, but she surely did. The more she was around him, the more she wanted him around. It made no sense at all, but she couldn't deny it. The truth of it sat heavily on her shoulders.

They traveled without incident and made it nearly to Grant land just as the sun was falling. She and Derric rode in the rear simply because their horses were more tired than the rest.

"You've overworked your mount, Dyna," Els said, listening to her horse's breathing.

"I know. 'Tis part of the reason I'm stopping. Derric and I both need fresh mounts. We worked these two too hard coming down the mountains. I should have slowed, but…"

"Don't second guess yourself, Diamond. We may never have caught them," Derric said. "You made a difference in the battle, even before your cousins came. Even before the spectral swords."

She gave him a quick look of appreciation, then

reined in her horse, slowing further. She yelled to her cousins, "We're on Grant land. I'm taking my horse to the burn, then we'll follow."

Alasdair shouted back, "Corbett, you'll stay with her."

Derric smiled, probably because the man who'd warned him away from Dyna was now asking him to stay by her side. It also didn't escape her notice that Alasdair rarely asked for things. He tossed out orders like Grandsire did, knowing they'd be followed.

She supposed serving as laird of MacLintock Castle, with Emmalin, had encouraged that practice.

Pointing off toward the burn, she moved off the main path into the woods. She climbed down and led her horse over to the bubbling burn, leaning over to wrap her arms around his neck as a gesture of appreciation. "You did a fine job, Mid-Four." They'd taken to naming Midnight's descendants by number, partly because all of the grandchildren had wanted a horse named Midnight.

"Mid-Four?" Derric asked.

"Aye, when we were younger, we argued about which of us were allowed to name a horse Midnight. Papa made sure I had one of his stallions, so I wished to name him after his powerful sire. But so did Alasdair. And Els and Alick quickly joined in our argument. Grandpapa came into the middle of us and whistled, ceasing our argument in a hurry. Then he pointed to Alasdair, 'Midnight One; Two for you, Els; Three for Alick. Dyna, you are the youngest, so your mount will be Midnight Four.' Alick and Els chose other names though. And he also gave me one of Midnight's daughters. I love Misty. She's sweet, but she tires easily."

Derric dismounted, patting his horse as he led him to the burn. When he came up next to Dyna's horse, he said, "You did a fine job, Mid-Four," he said, leaning over to whisper in the beast's ear. "You were right. 'Twas Alex Grant."

Dyna snorted. "Are you not a big soft one around horses. How did I never notice before? What else do I not know about you, Corbett?"

He stepped so close that she thought he was about to kiss her, but instead he leaned into her ear. "You'll learn someday how I can make you scream my name with desire."

That deserved another snort from her along with a snicker. "You cannot wait to prove yourself, can you?"

He smiled, kissed her cheek and moved over to the burn to wash his face. "You have a fine horse, Diamond, if he could pick up a man's scent that easily."

She leaned against a tree and slowly nodded, staring at her beloved horse who picked his head up to nicker as if to give his own input into the conversation. "But now that I think on it, Mid-Four probably smelled Grandsire's scent at the overlook. I'll bet he and Loki met there to talk. 'Tis Loki's favorite spot, too. When he was young, they'd have to drag him away from there."

Derric fussed over the two beasts a bit more

before giving her his full attention. "Bloody hell, but the power you cousins carry is a sight to see."

"I wish I could see it again from a different vantage point. It never lasts for long," she muttered. Then she shook her head. "I still can't believe that I failed Grandsire."

"How is it that you failed him?" He stood in front of her and brushed the back of his fingers across her cheek, her gaze locked on his.

"I was the one who knew he was in trouble. Do you not recall we were the ones who left Bruce's camp first? I should have been able to catch Busby. Stop the bastard from taking him." She massaged her forehead, sick with worry. Why hadn't she anticipated that Busby would ride off with him? "He's still out there with that sheriff."

"Do you not recall that Loki stopped you?"

She hadn't thought of that, but Derric was right. "True, but I still failed him. I—"

Dyna stopped, her eyes wide. They weren't alone. Turning around, she heard another sound. She held a finger to her lips to tell Derric to stay quiet.

No one from the clan would be out here, they were too far outside the gates. She grabbed her bow and started to stalk away from the burn.

"Diamond?" Derric whispered, but she waved him back.

Then she saw him.

A gray-haired man ran away from them, climbing onto his horse's back and heading in the opposite direction. Dyna ran back and leaped on her beast. "Sorry, Mid-Four," she said, "but we have someone to chase after."

"Who?" Derric shouted as he jumped on his horse to follow.

She yelled back to him over her shoulder. "My guess is that we've found my sister's stalker."

She pushed her horse and, to her surprise, caught up with the vagrant quickly. A few moments later, Derric appeared on the man's other side.

He was an old man with long gray hair and a gray beard, something that she hadn't expected at all. He had a decent mount so she guessed he wasn't a reiver.

So who the hell was he?

The man looked from Dyna to Derric and wisely slowed his horse, coming to a stop between the two.

"Who are you and what are you doing here?" Dyna shouted.

The man was breathing too hard to answer. He didn't speak quickly enough for her so Dyna reached over for the reins of his horse and said, "Fine. We'll see what the Grant lairds think of you. And you better hope you're not the man who's been watching us."

The man's shoulders slumped, but he still didn't say a word.

"What's your name?"

He didn't answer, just stared straight ahead.

"Answer me, fool," Dyna commanded.

"I'll not answer anyone until I see your laird and the mistress."

"What do you want with the laird?" If she had

her way, she'd slap the man until he spit out everything he knew.

The man stared straight ahead, and Derric said, "You best answer her or you're about to feel the point of my sword, old man."

Never looking at them, he muttered, "I'm on Grant land. One of the lairds is Connor Grant and his wife is Sela and they have a daughter named Claray. I came to see Sela. They know me."

Dyna gasped. Claray hadn't been imagining the man, after all. She'd always hoped her sister would be able to forget about the spiders one day. That she would find a man to marry so she could have bairns of her own. But the memories raged in her mind, tormenting her at unexpected times.

"You've been spying on my family!" she said. "I'll pin you to a tree by your bollocks for hurting my sister."

He offered neither a denial nor a retort, and Dyna felt a sudden gush of elation. Claray wasn't as sick as she'd feared, and she'd actually caught her sister's tormentor. When she made it to the gates, she said to the guards, "Open up. I have Claray's stalker."

Her prisoner said nothing, allowing her to lead the man into the keep. They rode past the stables, across the famous Grant courtyard, through the bailey, and came to a stop directly in front of the steps. Her sire appeared in front of her, Alasdair and Els behind him. "What the hell, daughter? Who is this man?"

"This is the man Claray saw watching her. I

caught him on the edge of our land, and he says he knows you and Mama."

Connor Grant stared at the man. "Your name?"

"I'd like to see your mistress first. Then I'll give you my name."

"Papa, don't listen to him. Bring Claray out, see if she recognizes him."

The man stared at Connor. "I met you once. You were on the way to Lochluin Abbey when I caught up with you. I came back to advise you that Hord had found his way back and was after Sela."

Something flickered in her sire's eyes, but he gave no indication that he believed the man. "Get him down," he said to Alasdair. "You and Els will guard him in the great hall, and I'll send for Sela and Claray."

"My thanks to you," the older man said. "'Tis all I want."

"I'll keep my eye on you the whole time," Dyna said, following her cousins as they escorted the man inside the keep. "I won't let you get away with anything." She would have argued with her sire that no additional escort was needed—that she could handle the situation given she'd found the man and brought him in—but a part of her knew he'd made the right decision.

She was too emotional. Too personally invested in the matter.

As she followed the others inside, Derric came up behind her, his hand on the small of her back. "Diamond, why don't you allow your sire to take charge?" he said softly. "He's laird, is he not?"

She glared at him but closed her mouth.

Her father, who had hung back to allow the lads to escort the stranger in first, said, "You've chosen a wise man, daughter. I know you think you're doing what's right, but you don't understand the situation. Allow your mother to offer her opinion."

They stepped inside the keep and her father sent all the servants out, asking one of them to fetch her mother and Claray.

Connor Grant questioned the man again while the servant left to retrieve them.

"Why are you here?"

The man nodded to the laird and said, "Forgive me, my lord, but I'm an old man. Before I leave this land, I had to make sure they were safe and well. I didn't wish to bring up any bad memories or cause trouble. I was planning to leave on the morrow. You've taken good care of Sela and Claray. 'Twas all I wanted to know. If I could just speak with Sela, 'tis my only request. I promise I'll take my leave after that."

Dyna listened but couldn't make any sense of his words. This man had implied he was from her mother's past, yet to her knowledge, all of the men who'd harmed and manipulated her mother were dead. So who was this man?

Her mother appeared at the balcony with Claray, and her sister let out a scream, her hands flying up to cover her mouth. When she recovered a wee bit, she pointed at the gray-haired man.

"'Tis him! Mama, 'tis the man I saw outside the gates. He was watching me. Mama…"

Sela Grant squared her shoulders as she peered down at the intruder. "Stay here," she said to Claray, squeezing her shoulder. Then she descended the stairs, as regal as any queen in her castle, her blue gown trailing behind her. Her eyes never left the intruder.

When her feet met the bottom of the staircase, she stopped, still staring at the man.

"Sela, I just had to see how you were," the old man said. Tears fell down his cheeks. "See if dear Claray was hale. I'll pass on soon, but I had to know."

Sela strode over to stand in front of him. "Vern?" she asked, her voice revealing that she did, in fact, know him.

He nodded. "You're as beautiful as ever, my lady."

Dyna watched in mute shock as her mother reached for her father's arm. "This is Vern. He's the man who protected Claray when Hord kept her captive." She reached up to cup the old man's cheek. "He kept an eye on her and always let me know how she was doing."

Connor nodded. "I thought I recognized him, but I needed to hear it from you." He turned to a serving lass and said, "Get a trencher and an ale for our guest."

Claray crept down the steps, her eyes on Vern, her hands not releasing their tight grip on the railing. Tears poured down her cheeks as she made her way over to him. She came to a stop a few steps behind Sela, her hand on their mother's elbow. "Mama?"

Dyna couldn't watch any more. "Mama, this man has been *watching* Claray. Mayhap he was going to kidnap her, steal her away from you. He's guilty of causing her many sleepless nights." Horrified that her parents were welcoming this vagrant into their home, her voice reached a feverish pitch she didn't even recognize. "The nightmares came back, she thought the spiders were back."

The look in her mother's eye—her look of ice, or so Dyna's father had always called it—stopped her mid-sentence. Her mother never looked at her like that. She stepped back until her legs hit a bench at the trestle table.

"Dyna, this man saved me from death, and he saved your sister from Hord. If not for Vern, we would not be here, *you* would not be here."

Vern's gaze shot from Dyna to Sela and then settled on Claray. "I just wanted to know that you were both hale. I'm sorry, Claray, if I frightened you. I didn't realize you'd seen me. I didn't think you'd remember me. You were so young when Hord held you captive." He moved to a chair and sat down, his breathing labored. "They told me I have less than six moons before I pass, that I should take any last journeys now. I had to see you, Sela. I should have come to the door, but I meant what I said. I didn't wish to upset anyone."

Dyna fell onto the bench beneath her, so confused she didn't know what to think. Had she gotten everything wrong again? Dyna wasn't used to her impulses steering her wrong, but that's all they seemed to do lately.

Claray reached for the old man's hand. "I remember your voice." She looked at her mother and said, "'Tis not a clear memory, but there's something about his voice that is soothing."

"Because they kept you from your mama, and I often rocked you to sleep. I'll leave you now. I've seen what I needed to. Claray, you are a beautiful lass, and I hope you've been able to get past all that happened to you. I did what I could to help you both."

Her father pulled out a chair and said, "Nay, Vern, you'll stay the night with us. Welcome to Clan Grant. I'm grateful to you for all you did for my family, and for telling me about Hord. I made sure the bastard would never torture Sela or Claray again."

Suddenly, it was all too much. Dyna had made a mistake, and her grandsire was still missing, and apparently the only person she'd saved Claray from was someone who was fond of her. Emotions rushed through her, bubbling over, and tears streamed down her face. She sobbed and sobbed because all her efforts had come to naught. She hadn't saved anyone.

Derric strode over and lifted her into his arms, and she buried her face into his shoulder. He carried her to the door of the keep, but he stopped on the threshold and said, "Dyna, your sire is here and would like to speak with you."

She lifted her head from Derric's shoulder and looked at her sire. "I'm sorry, Papa."

"For what? You've done naught wrong. I think

you're exhausted. Derric, take her up to her chamber and she can sleep."

"Nay," Dyna said, gripping Derric's arm. "I'd rather sleep under a tree outside the gates. Please, Papa. I cannot be in here right now."

"As you wish. Take care of her, Corbett. I've sent three patrols out, and we'll be sending several more patrols for my sire in the morn. Rest up, Dyna. We need you."

Once they were near the stables, Dyna said, "Derric, take me away from here."

He lifted her onto a fresh mount, grabbed the reins of another horse that had already been saddled, and mounted behind her. Alasdair waved them on.

They rode out through the gates and headed off Grant land.

Dyna said, "Find me a place to sleep, then I'm going after Grandsire."

"I had a feeling that's what your plan was, Diamond."

"I failed my sister, but I'll not fail my grandfather. I cannot wait until morn."

CHAPTER TWENTY-FOUR

DERRIC FOUND A SPOT UNDER a tree and placed several furs under it, settling Dyna on it. She fell asleep before he finished settling the horses.

He sighed, staring at the lass he loved, a feeling so deep and all-encompassing he could scarcely believe it. Right now, she was too exhausted and heart-sore to recognize what she'd accomplished by finding Claray's stalker. The situation may not have been what she'd expected, but she'd allowed her sister to put a crushing fear behind her, plus she'd forced Vern to reveal himself, something he clearly hadn't intended to do.

If he were to guess, Dyna was probably more upset about the look her mother had given her in the hall. They'd sort it out—he'd never seen a closer and more loving family than the Grants. The bigger question, for him, was why Connor had given Derric leave to take Dyna outside the gates.

But he thought he might know the answer to that, too. Knowing Dyna as he did, Connor had likely known damn well that she would get up in the middle of the night and go after her grandsire. By encouraging Derric to escort her, he'd guaranteed there would be at least one person to assist her.

Connor Grant was a wise man.

And he hoped he would have the chance to ask the man if he had his approval to marry his daughter. That is, if Dyna agreed. She was a stubborn lass.

He fell asleep with a smile on his face.

Less than an hour later, he awakened feeling an arousal stronger than anything he'd ever experienced. He looked down, surprised to see a hand had snaked underneath his trews and was stroking him.

Dyna gave him a wicked smile when he looked up at her. "Diamond, if you keep that up, we'll finish. This will not be one-sided either. You will finish."

She let her hand drop from his hardened sex and removed her tunic, tossing it off to the side. Moonlight bathed her breasts in a soft glow, and he couldn't stop himself for reaching for her, but she stepped back.

"You're a tease, are you?"

She smiled and slid her leggings down over her legs with a wriggle, turning sideways to give him a tantalizing view of her bottom before she stepped out of her clothing, now gloriously nude.

He was out of his trews in a second, and he whipped off his tunic and tugged her close, wrapping his arms around her so they were skin to skin.

"So you wish to finish this, lass?"

"Aye, I do. I love you, Derric Corbett, and I wish to be with you always. Handfast with me?" she said, running her hands across his bulging biceps.

"I thought the man was supposed to ask the woman to marry. Or are you balking convention again?"

She grinned. "You did not answer. Accept or reject my proposal first."

"Naught would please me more. Will you marry me, Dyna Grant?"

"Aye. It is done. Now finish this."

His lips captured hers in a searing kiss, his tongue parting her lips so he could taste all of her. Groaning, he pulled back. "Bloody hell, Diamond. You're enough to drive a man daft. Do you know how many times I've thought of this? Thought of how I hurt you, how I wronged you?"

"'Tis as I said. You didn't wrong me."

"But—"

She pressed a finger to his lips. "I want you. Now."

He smoothed a plaid on the ground, and she lowered herself onto it, bringing him with her. Derric was on top of her, but he hadn't settled himself between her thighs yet. Determined to give her pleasure first, he whispered, "I promise you'll not want to push me away this time. It should not hurt."

"Derric, I need to see this finished. I need to know what 'tis like."

He kissed her again, slanting his mouth over hers, then he trailed a line of kisses down her neck to her breast, suckling one and kneading the other as she arched against him.

Her hands roamed his body, his buttocks, his hips, his upper arms, something he found highly arousing. Her need was as great as his, which gave him an idea—he rolled onto his back and settled her on top. She stared down at him for a moment, questioning his move. "Diamond, you'll be in control."

"But I don't know what to do."

"You'll figure it out. Kiss me," he said, his hand going to the vee between her legs, pleased to find her slick with need already. He thrust a finger inside her liquid heat and swallowed her gasp. He couldn't stop from moaning as her passion reached a feverish pitch from his caresses. His hands found her backside and caressed her there as he eased her over him.

"Take me in your hand, Diamond. You're ready for me. Slide me inside."

She positioned his tip, testing it carefully. He guessed she was fearful that it would hurt like it had last time, so he allowed her to move slowly, taking him inside a bit more with each thrust, her hand still on him.

Once he was halfway inside her, she spread her legs wider and leveraged herself just right to take all of him inside, burying him in so deeply that he grasped her hips.

"Dyna, you will drive me over the edge too quickly. Slow down," he whispered. She did, for a time, moving carefully over him, even testing different angles, but then she picked up the pace with a rhythmic pulsing that drove him mad and made them both breathless.

"Derric, please. What do I do? I don't know how to…"

He touched a spot above where they were joined, rubbing her until she screamed, convulsing against him, her head thrown back with such pleasure that he knew she'd finally finished. He grasped her hips to get her exactly where he wanted her, then climaxed with a roar as he exploded inside her.

She fell against him, her breathing ragged as she chuckled.

"I had no idea."

He laughed against her, his hands still on the tight cheeks of her bottom, holding himself inside her. "So you finished this time, Diamond?"

Her hot breath came out in a whoosh against his neck. "Aye, and so did you, Corbett."

"Are you sure?"

"Absolutely. I only have one complaint."

"What? I didn't please you?" he asked, caressing her bottom.

"Oh, you pleased me completely. Why the hell didn't you make me finish before?"

CHAPTER TWENTY-FIVE

DYNA WOKE UP, STILL SMILING from their lovemaking. She knew Derric was going to get upset with her, but she wasn't going to awaken him. She dressed quietly, took care of her needs, then led her horse out of the area before she mounted, heading out into the Highlands to find her grandfather.

Her horse nickered as if to remind her she forgot someone. "You like him better than me. 'Tis that not the truth of it?" Couldn't blame the animal for all the sweet-talking Derric did to the horses— all of them. Stopping the beast, she thought again about her dream and how she hadn't been the one who'd rescued her grandsire.

It had been Derric. Changing her mind, she turned her horse around to go back for him, surprised to find him heading her way as soon as she went around the bend. Pulling up short, she wasn't surprised when Derric spoke to her sharply.

"You thought you'd sneak away from me again? I was waiting for you this time, Diamond."

She slowed her horse, allowing him to come closer. "I thought of waking you, but you were sleeping peacefully. I only planned to go a short way before I returned for you. But I changed my mind. Can you not see I just came back for you?"

"Lying does not become you, lass," he drawled.

Dyna broke into a peal of laughter and sent her horse flying across the meadow, leaving Derric behind her. Truth was, she was glad he'd joined her. This was not the time to go off on her own. She slowed her horse again and said, "Do you think you can keep up with me, old man?"

Derric hollered, "You'll pay for that later."

She laughed, and for a few minutes they raced on their horses, Dyna enjoying the wind in her face, but the seriousness of their mission set in as soon as they were off Grant land.

"Diamond, wait," Derric called from behind her.

She slowed enough for him.

"Do you have a plan or are we wandering aimlessly?"

"Sometimes I travel based on my intuition. 'Tis what will guide me today." Her gaze searched the area all the while they spoke, looking for anything to trigger her special talents. Anything that would have meaning for her grandfather.

"I'll accept that for a while, but if we find nothing, we'll need a new plan."

She couldn't argue with that reasoning, and besides, she felt certain they *would* find something. In fact, she suspected they would find that cottage she'd seen in her vision days before. This was the day she'd predicted.

There were multiple patrols out, but they didn't know the Highlands the way she did, nor did they have her abilities as a seer. Sometimes the knowledge came to her so clearly, it was like someone whispering in her ear. It was like that now, and she knew precisely which way to go, almost as if a hand rose and pointed in the correct direction at every crossroads she reached.

They traveled for about two hours before she felt guided off the regular path, to a familiar cottage. It was the one she'd seen in her vision. She pointed to it, leading Derric there as quietly as possible.

Smoke came out of the chimney, indicating someone was there. They left their horses tied to a bush and crept closer, not completely surprised to trip over something along the way.

The arm of a dead man. Busby.

So her grandsire was alone with another captor.

Dyna said, "I'm going inside. You stand watch out here. We don't know where the other man is yet." Something told her she should allow Derric to go first because it would fit with her dream, but she couldn't wait. This had to be where he was being held.

Derric nodded and drew his sword, making his way around the cottage carefully.

Creeping as stealthily as she could, she made her way toward the closest window, listening for any evidence of who might be inside. She waited just beside the window, out of sight, and although she didn't hear anything, she was able to shift the wooden shutter slightly. It was enough.

Grandsire lay on his back on a pallet, and he looked dead.

Her hand came up to her mouth to cover her gasp. She didn't see anyone else around, so she moved quietly to the door, opening it quietly and peering around for anyone, her dagger in hand, but the place looked empty. Abandoned. Alex Grant's long legs hung over the end of the short, makeshift bed.

"Grandsire," she cried, flying to his side and dropping to her knees, praying it wasn't so. "Grandsire, wake up." She prodded him, shook his hand, poked his shoulder, but he didn't move.

Devastated, she recalled something Alasdair had told her. "Hold your hand in front of their nose or mouth to see if they still breathe. If they're hurt or injured, it will be slow, but you'll still feel it." Poor Alasdair knew from experience, having lost both of his parents, one after the other.

She held her palm under grandsire's nose, fingers pressed to his upper lip, and thought she felt a small breath. Her hand reached to his forehead. He was still warm, which was a good thing, but then she noticed something she hadn't seen from the window.

His hands were tied together and he'd been beaten. His eye was black and crusted over with blood. He had bruises on a cheek, and a cut lip that had swollen up. She released his bindings, but he never reacted to her touch.

Dyna did the only thing she could think to do.

She rested her head on his upper body and sobbed. "Grandsire," she whispered. "Please come back to me. I'm not ready to lose you yet."

He still didn't move. She put her ear to his chest, hoping to hear a heartbeat, but it was difficult to listen over her sobs. No matter how she tried, she couldn't stop her tears.

She didn't hear him until he grabbed her from behind in a bear hug.

"I knew you'd come inside. He's not dead yet, but he will be soon."

She sliced the man's arm with her dagger, dark blood spurting out from the wound, but he knocked it away and cursed her.

"Bitch!" He dragged her over to a chair and tried to tie her to it while she kicked and bit at him, doing everything she could to fight him off. "My, but you are a feisty one, are you not? Wait until I get you in my bed."

She fought with all her strength and shouted first Derric's name and then her grandsire's. This is why the dream showed Derric as the one to save him. She would be useless tied up. "Derric, hurry! The bastard is in here!"

Her captor slapped her three times to silence her, then tossed her on the floor. He tried throwing himself on top of her, but she kneed him in his groin and shoved him off of her.

"Slap me, hit me, all you want," she seethed, "but you'll never stop me. I'll kill you, but not before I thrust my dagger between your legs, you bastard."

She grabbed the dagger up off the floor, but

the man had clambered to his feet again, and he knocked it away from her. Then he yanked her head back by the plait so he could stare at her. "I was going to pay him back, but you don't look anything like her. Your eyes are the wrong shade of blue, your hair is too light. I grabbed the wrong one. There is one who looks just like Maddie."

"You're a slimy piece of shite," she ground out. "Why in hell would any woman want you? You smell and look like an overstuffed pig. You make me gag."

That put him over the edge. He grabbed her hair and held a dagger to her throat, then bellowed so loudly Derric was sure to hear him if he hadn't already heard her. "Who is she? Who's the one who looks like Maddie? Tell me, or I'll cut your grandfather's throat right in front of you."

Dyna spat in his face.

He cursed and grabbed a chair, throwing her into it. "I think I'll have my fun with you before I kill you."

Derric woke up with a raging headache, confirmed by the knot in the back of his head and the crusted blood on his neck. He sat up to get his bearings and noticed a large rock not far from him, speckles of blood on it. "I can't believe that didn't kill me." His next thought was that it knocked him daft because he was talking to himself. He rubbed his head again, winced, and glanced around him, surprised to see no one at all.

Where the hell was Dyna?

As soon as he heard her scream, he stood up and headed to the cottage. "Bloody hell, Diamond. There's never a dull moment with you."

He approached the window of the cottage. Peeking through it, he saw Dyna tied to a chair, held captive by a man who waved a dagger about screaming something about Maddie.

While he wished to charge in like a fool and attack the bastard, he knew better. The element of surprise was his best weapon. He'd wait until the man had his back to the door, then rush him and a plunge a sword into his back, aiming for a kidney. Not the most sporting approach, but the man had imprisoned his wife. He wasn't taking chances.

He moved to the closed door and opened it just a touch, wanting a better look at the scene he would be entering. The kidnapper was a large man with a small protruding belly. He guessed him to be around five decades old, something that surprised him.

Alex Grant lay motionless on a pallet at the back of the cottage. Derric closed his eyes and prayed the Grant patriarch wasn't dead. Dyna would never cease to blame herself if she lost him like this. Mayhap he was a fool to wait. They needed to get Alex to a healer.

He was about to rush in when he heard Alex's voice. "Hamish, you're a daft fool. Maddie never loved you."

"You're lying. You ruined everything." Derric heard scuffling feet and then another sound that he suspected was a chair scraping across the floor, though he couldn't imagine why. Where was he dragging her if she was tied to the chair?

Alex began to yell again to draw the man's attention from Dyna, shouting, "Maddie thought you were a sad fool, Hamish. Aye, the only emotion she felt toward you was pity. If you hadn't left, I would have killed you for approaching her, you bastard."

Hamish erupted, which gave Derric exactly the opportunity he'd been waiting for. He swung the door open and charged Hamish from behind, aiming his dagger at the man's broad back. And mayhap it would have worked if the bastard hadn't swung around and cut Derric's arm, causing him to drop the dagger instantly. The man kicked him in his bollocks so hard he thought he would vomit.

There was naught he could do but fall to the floor. His vision dimmed and he fought to keep his eyes open.

No, no, no.

It seemed as if everything that could have gone wrong had. If he didn't do something soon, the future he saw with Dyna—the life of love and laughter and the little bairns with yellow hair— it would never happen. With Dyna's hands bound behind a chair and Derric incapacitated on the floor, their captor was firmly in control of the situation. It didn't matter that Derric would be stronger than him in a man-to-man fight, or that Dyna could shoot ten arrows from a treetop.

Derric gagged, holding his arm in an attempt to stop the bleeding, then coughed to draw the man's attention away from Dyna. "You think you can hold her down? She's tougher than you'll ever be, you ugly old bastard." Hellfire, his bollocks hurt. He did his best to push himself to his knees, but it was a struggle.

The man called Hamish spun around and tried to kick him, but Dyna tripped the man, her glorious long legs knocking him to the floor in an instant. Hamish's head hit the stone hard.

So hard it knocked him out, which would have been excellent if not for one problem.

The man had fallen directly on top of Derric, knocking him back down onto the floor and pinning him. He landed with an oof, the tumble leaving him breathless for a moment. "Well done, wife," he said between breaths, trying unsuccessfully to move the unconscious man. "But couldn't you have pushed him the other way?"

"Pardon me, husband, but if you have not noticed, my hands are tied." She hopped in her chair, trying to get closer to Derric.

"Kick him off me, the big piece of lard is dead weight. He'll suffocate me for sure."

"I'm trying," she mumbled, jumping with her chair.

"Hurry because my bollocks still hurt. I don't know if I can heave enough to move him off of me."

"Oh, for heaven's sake, Derric. They're just hairy sacs. Can you not just suck it up? Why must you act like they're made of gold?" She made it over to Derric and managed to put both feet on Hamish and push.

Derric gritted his teeth and said, "They're harder than boulders right now, Diamond, but they may get squished to naught if you don't help me. If that happens, there'll be no bairns for us." He gritted his teeth, ignored the pain in his sacs, and pushed for all he was worth at the same time. "And my arm is still bleeding, or haven't you noticed?"

"Quit crying like a bairn," she said through gritted teeth.

"Crying like a bairn? How would you feel in my place?"

"I'd still be able to push harder than that. What happened to your muscles?" she asked as she clenched her jaw. "I have to get my feet underneath him somehow. Can you move him with what few muscles you have?"

"My muscles are buried under the flab and fat of an old man, doing their best to crush the breath out of me."

The two pushed at the same time and a sudden storm erupted outside the cottage, flashing bolts of lightning illuminating the hut just before a heavy downpour started. At the same exact time, the two managed to heave together and pushed Hamish off of Derric, sending him airborne quite a distance. Derric rolled over onto his side, gasping for air. "I thought the bastard was going to suffocate me."

"Untie me, husband."

Derric could barely see straight, but he managed to find the dagger on the floor and cut her free. She threw her arms around his neck and said, "My thanks for saving me."

Derric nuzzled her neck, grateful to have her in his arms. "I think you saved me, Diamond."

A voice from behind him said, "So you two are supposed to save Scotland? I'm going to have to ask Maddie about this."

"Grandsire! You're hale." Dyna rushed to his side and hugged him tight.

But the old man pushed her back and said, "Dyna, would you like to explain to me how you know what his bollocks look like?"

Derric quickly stepped in front of her and asked, "Alex, may I have your approval to marry your granddaughter? We handfasted, and we both agreed to abide by it, but I would like your approval of the match. Though I'd also like your approval to chew her arse out for leaving without more guards."

"That depends. Did you meet your quest?"

"What quest?" Dyna asked, her head jerking from one face to the other.

"Never mind," her grandsire said. "I posed the question to Corbett."

"Aye, I've seen it more than once. With her sister and especially with you. You opened my eyes."

Alex gave him a stern look, but followed it with a nod. "Then you have my approval, Corbett, but she'll get an arse-chewing from more than one person. You can count on it."

"Fine. Chew my arse out. At least we found you," Dyna said, staring at her beloved grandfather and kissing his cheek. "I thought you were dead."

"Nay, I'm fine, lass. He gave me a potion to make

me sleep. 'Twas hard to stay awake. You may have to help me get on a horse, though. He did a fine job battering me."

"We'll do whatever it takes, Grandsire."

"Is the bastard still alive?" He tipped his head toward Hamish on the floor.

She moved back, leaned down, and placed her hands at his neck to see if his heart still beat. "I think the fall killed him. I cannot feel anything."

"Shall I bury him?" Derric asked, noting the man's color was turning a dusky gray.

"Leave the bastard there. I'll send a few guards back when I find some," Alex said.

She stopped for a moment and said, "What did you mean by you having to ask Maddie? When did you see her? Have you had another dream?"

Derric rubbed the stubble on his chin. "And what was that comment about saving Scotland?"

Alex sighed, pushing himself to a standing position, though it was clearly a struggle, so they both rushed to his sides to assist him. "I had a dream a while ago. Maddie said you were the last important piece to the spectral swords, Derric. Did you not hear the heavens explode when the two of you combined your efforts to get Hamish off of Derric? Or how high you tossed his body into the air? You had some assistance in that endeavor."

"What?" Dyna asked in surprise as her grandsire pushed her away, walked around her, and headed toward the door.

"The heavens exploded?" Derric muttered, looking at his wife. He'd missed something, clearly, though he had to admit he had been quite focused on the state of his poor bollocks. Not that anyone cared.

"When you combined forces, the heavens rewarded you," Alex said over his shoulder as he stepped through the door. Then he stopped to turn back and look at them. "And the storm stopped as quickly as it started."

Derric had no idea what the man was talking about.

"You should remember that." He tipped his head and left, a sudden rainbow appearing in the sky behind him.

Derric and Dyna stared at each other, mouths agape.

Dyna whispered, "What if he's right?"

CHAPTER TWENTY-SIX

THEY ARRIVED BACK ON GRANT land to a parade of escorts, waiting for them on horseback. Not that Dyna was surprised. They'd run into a patrol on the way back and sent some ahead to bring word to the family while Alex sent some back to the cottage to bury Hamish.

Alasdair and Emmalin, Els and Joya, and Alick and Branwen were there, as was Chrissa, who squealed at the sight of them. The path was lined by clan members, including both lairds and Aunt Kyla, her mother and siblings all waving to them as they moved on, though there were tears on many cheeks. Seeing them all waiting, smiles on their faces, filled her with so much emotion that she couldn't bring herself to ride forward.

Leaning over to her grandsire, who'd recovered enough to ride his own horse, she said in an undertone, "I love you, Grandpapa. And I love Derric, too. Thank you for accepting him into our family."

The great warrior passed her, but still, she held back, allowing the rest of her family to celebrate his return. Then Derric rode up to greet his sister. He said something softly to her, and Dyna couldn't help but wonder if it had something to do their marriage. She hoped so. But still, she didn't move.

Dyna's father greeted Grandsire, but then he rode straight to her. "Your mother will ask me. Why are you holding back?"

She burst into tears, surprised to feel so much emotion so close to the surface. "I love you, Papa, and I love Derric. We handfasted, and I don't wish for a wedding. I just wish to enjoy our marriage."

Her father smiled and leaned over to kiss her cheek. "I'm happy for you, daughter. If Derric still had the courage to pursue you after all we did to frighten him away, then he is worthy of being your husband. My thanks for being bold enough to find your grandfather. None of us are ready to lose him yet."

Grandsire yelled back, "They're quite entertaining together. You'll see."

Dyna blushed a deep shade of red, not willing to admit her grandsire had overheard her talking about her husband's sacs.

"Do you wish to tell me what he meant by that?"

She shook her head. "Probably best if he tells you, Papa. For now, I wish to enjoy my new husband. My thanks for accepting him. I do love him, Papa, and he loves me."

"He'd have to be special in order to keep up with you. Your mother and I always said it would take a special man. We both welcome him into Clan

Grant."

"He is. You'll see." The cheers and warm wishes carried to them and she could only smile, waving her sire on to share in the celebration.

"I look forward to spending more time with him." Her father tipped his head to her and went after his father.

She dismounted then, patting her horse as she allowed her tears to flow freely, something she rarely did. The others had started riding back to the castle, but Derric noticed and he stopped his horse. He dismounted and hurried over to her. "Diamond, I don't think I've ever seen you cry so much."

She grinned through her tears. "Because I usually don't cry. I know I did over Claray and Grandsire, but that was the first time in a long time. I'm not crying now."

He moved over to stand in front of her, brushing his hand across her wet cheek. "I think you need to touch your cheek. Those are distinctly tears." He gave her a lopsided grin.

Dyna couldn't control her emotions any longer. She launched herself at her husband and said, "I love you, Derric Corbett. I'm so glad you're my husband."

He kissed her tenderly. "I love you, too, Dyna Grant. Will you stay with me forever? I have this fear you'll run away from me because you're such a powerful warrior."

"I'll not leave you. Do you mind if we live here on Grant land for a while?"

"I'd like that. I need to speak with your sire. I'll ask if he'd like to have a wedding in front of everyone."

Her head was already shaking. "Nay, we married right over there." She pointed off to the clearing. "And I wouldn't change it for the world. I'll remember it forever. He'll accept it."

He arched a brow at her. "And your mother and your siblings?"

"My mother will accept it. She feared I'd never find someone who would put up with my eccentricities, but I did. We'll stay here until Scotland needs us, and then we'll go fight, just like we've done all along."

He nuzzled her neck and said, "I'd like that. You need to know I'd never try to change you, Diamond. I love you exactly as you are."

"What do you mean by that?" She wasn't sure whether it was a compliment.

"I love you even though you fight better than most men, you're a wee bit too blunt at times, and you wear men's clothing. And I love that you have a soft heart."

She couldn't help but snort. "I don't have a soft heart."

"A wise old man warned me to stay away from you unless I could complete his quest."

"Grandsire? What exactly was that quest?"

"I had to get to know your soft heart or I couldn't have your hand in marriage."

"Grandsire said that?"

"Aye. I'll admit it took a while."

"But I don't have a soft…"

Derric pressed a finger to his lips. "You just cried over a reception for the return of your grandfather, did you not?"

"Nay, 'tis not why I cried," she replied, squeezing his forearms.

"Then why?"

"Because I love you so much, and I feared the same thing my mother did. I didn't think I'd ever find a man who'd accept a wife who wears leggings all the time."

"Well, I'd rather see you differently…"

She playfully slapped his arm, a fierce scowl on her face. "I like my leggings."

He whispered, "I'd rather see you with them off."

EPILOGUE

Seven years later, The Highlands of Scotland

AVELINA SAT UP, AWOKEN BY a premonition so strong, she immediately got out of bed, leaving her husband, Drew, to sleep. A buttery gold light shone outside her window, so she donned a robe and padded down to the courtyard, careful not to awaken the others in their keep.

As soon as she stepped outside, the entire area was basked in golden light. A gorgeous woman in a lavender and yellow gown appeared to float down from the sky, surrounded by butterflies. The shock of it lasted only a moment before a smile crossed Avelina's face. It had been a long, long time since she'd last had such a visitation.

Her brother Logan, who'd arrived the previous day for a visit, came out to stand behind her. "What the hell is that?"

"Don't you mean *who* is that? 'Tis Erena, the queen of the fae."

"Greetings, my dear. And I feel it's perfect that

your brother is here. He will have to help you in this endeavor. He's been gifted a very long life just so he'd be here to assist you." Erena held her arms up to the skies and the swarm of butterflies all flapped their wings at the same time.

"What endeavor, Erena?" Avelina asked.

"Evil is in Scotland again. We'd hoped it would take care of itself, but it has not, so we must intervene."

"How am I to help?"

"You must find the sapphire sword. Do you recall where you hid it?"

"Aye."

"You must take it to Alex Grant in the Highlands. You know of him, correct?"

"Aye. His sister married my dear brother, Quade, God rest his soul."

"Logan will escort you to Grant land. You will give the sapphire sword to Alex Grant. He will know who he is to give it to, do not worry."

"But part of the legend of the sapphire sword is that the person who holds it must marry within two months of the date they received it. Must we tell them of this? Is that still the requirement?"

Erena shook her head. "Nay, this one is too young and besides, he's already found his mate in life. But he'll protect the weapon, fear not. Alex Grant will tell you all. Godspeed to you. I'll be watching your journey, so if there is any trouble, you can call upon me."

With that, she waved her arms and disappeared.

Avelina turned to her brother. "Are you hale

enough to go with me?"

"Of course. Think you I would allow you to see Alex Grant without me? And deliver the sword?" Logan snorted. "'Tis only right that the queen of the fae assigned me to escort you."

Alex Grant sat on a stool overlooking his land, taking in the sweet breeze and the smell of pines. The parapets were still his favorite place, although he could no longer come up on his own. The young people helped him get up the many steps.

He closed his eyes, overtired from his long day. "Maddie, is it no' my time yet?"

Maddie came to him and said, "It won't be long now, but you have one more task. You must help Logan Ramsay pass the sapphire sword along to its next owner. He and Lina will be along soon."

"But to whom?"

"You'll know," she said, kissing him deeply before she disappeared.

Alex opened his eyes, staring out over his lands. He searched for Maddie, the vision of her so real he swore he could smell her scent.

The clouds overhead began to swirl, bolts of lightning striking different spots in the landscape. A ferocious storm was on its way, so he moved to the door as quickly as he could. The door opened as he approached it. Derric and Dyna stood on the other side, Alick behind them.

"Grandsire, we've come to bring you back down," Alick said. "This storm will be nasty."

Alick and Derric lifted him together, ready to carry him down the steps but Alex said, "Wait."

They set him down and he stood, hanging on to their shoulders to support himself in the wind.

"Why do you wish to wait, Grandsire?" Alick asked.

"This storm. It looks the same as one I saw many years ago. The legend of the sapphire sword. She's right. The time has come. It hasn't been fifty years yet, but there's no denying there is evil here."

Derric shook his head and shot a wary look at Dyna. "Does he know of what he speaks?"

Dyna said, "I've heard the legend. Many years ago, an evil spirit found the sword, stole it away, and tried to kill many undeserving people, including Avelina Ramsay. The Queen of the Fae, a woman named Erena, came to Avelina and told her to find it and steal it back. The fae do not want it in the hands of evil."

"But what is the purpose of the sapphire sword?"

"I don't know if I can answer that, but Grandsire will tell you that the forces of the Grants and the Ramsays had to protect Avelina to save the sword, supposedly because it can have special powers. Grandpapa always speaks of it being a powerful storm unlike any other. But 'twas so long ago. Does she still hold the sword, Grandsire?"

"Aye, she still has it or knows where 'tis hidden. She married Drew Menzie. It hasn't been fifty years yet, but if the evil is strong enough, it could take place."

"But who will she give it to?"

"I think I know." The old man smiled, tipping his face up to the wind. "'Tis time."

THE END

DEAR READER,
     Thank you for continuing on this journey with the grandbairns of Alexander Grant, my fictitious warrior who fought in the Battle of Largs and also helped Robert the Bruce. His role and the stories of any Grants are products of my mind, but I tried to stay close to history for King Robert's part in the story, though his words are my own.

I have one more story planned in The Highland Swords, and after that, possibly a Christmas novella, then I'll be off to continue the stories of the other Grants and Ramsays: Elizabeth, Kenzie, Gillie, Padraig, Jennet, Brigid, and so many more.

Happy reading!

Keira Montclair

www.keiramontclair.com
www.facebook.com/KeiraMontclair
www.pinterest.com/KeiraMontclair

OTHER NOVELS BY KEIRA MONTCLAIR

FALLING FOR THE CHIEFTAIN-3RD in a
collaborative trilogy

THE SUMMERHILL SERIES- CON-TEMPORARY ROMANCE

ABOUT THE AUTHOR

KEIRA MONTCLAIR IS THE PEN name of an author who lives in South Carolina with her husband. She loves to write fast-paced, emotional romance, especially with children as secondary characters.

When she's not writing, she loves to spend time with her grandchildren. She's worked as a high school math teacher, a registered nurse, and an office manager. She loves ballet, mathematics, puzzles, learning anything new, and creating new characters for her readers to fall in love with.

She writes historical romantic suspense. Her bestselling series is a family saga that follows two medieval Scottish clans through three generations and now numbers over thirty books.

Contact her through her website,
www.keiramontclair.com.